The Millinery Bakers Detective Agency

The Millinery Bakers Detective Agency

SECRET SANTA SLAYS SIX

ALISON FORTUNE

Copyright © 2024 Alison Fortune

The moral right of the author has been asserted.

Apart from any fair dealing for the purposes of research or private study, or criticism or review, as permitted under the Copyright, Designs and Patents Act 1988, this publication may only be reproduced, stored or transmitted, in any form or by any means, with the prior permission in writing of the publishers, or in the case of reprographic reproduction in accordance with the terms of licences issued by the Copyright Licensing Agency. Enquiries concerning reproduction outside those terms should be sent to the publishers.

This is a work of fiction. Names, characters, businesses, places, events and incidents are either the products of the author's imagination or used in a fictitious manner. Any resemblance to actual persons, living or dead, or actual events is purely coincidental.

Troubador Publishing Ltd
Unit E2 Airfield Business Park,
Harrison Road, Market Harborough,
Leicestershire LE16 7UL
Tel: 0116 279 2299
Email: books@troubador.co.uk
Web: www.troubador.co.uk

ISBN 978 1 80514 469 4

British Library Cataloguing in Publication Data.
A catalogue record for this book is available from the British Library.

Printed and bound in Great Britain by 4edge Limited
Typeset in 11pt Minion Pro by Troubador Publishing Ltd, Leicester, UK

*With grateful thanks to my millinery consultant.
You know who you are.*

Introduction

Welcome to the Millinery Bakers Detective Agency. Run by Delores Marshall, milliner and owner of 'Hats with Attitude' and Agnes Trevin, baker and owner of 'Bring On The Cake'.

Set in the not-so-quiet Norfolk countryside, expertly assisted by their secret intelligence network. A nationwide team of elite, crack squad Women's Club members. Sure, some of these seventy-ninety-plus-year-olds look sweet and innocent but has anyone ever wondered why they have talks on military manoeuvres and has no one really questioned their recent day trip to MI5?

One

Esme

At eighty-five years of age, Esme Smith was considered a redoubtable marvel by her family.

Fiercely independent, financially savvy, still living in her own home of some sixty-three years, a fine cook, expert gardener, and family champion of every board game at Christmas.

The only concession Esme made to her age was a twice-weekly cleaner who came in and gave the place a good polish, a thorough vacuum in every room, did all the laundry and ironing, and scrubbed everything from ceiling to floor. Esme's house sparkled.

The cleaner had been recommended to Esme by her friend, Edith. Esme had long been impressed at how much Edith's flat sparkled and shone and smelt oh so sweet, so Esme didn't hesitate when Edith offered her the cleaner's number. Esme's son and Edith's far-away niece were quietly relieved that someone was coming in to 'do' for their respective elderly relatives' homes as it was one less thing to worry about.

Of course, neither Esme nor Edith told their families that their cleaner, Max, was from a company called 'Barely There Cleaning' whose tag line was *We Clean to Give You Pleasure*, where the cleaners provided were young males dressed only in budgie smugglers only just covering their gentlemen's regalia. The cleaning company had been set up to redress the balance in that just because you were an *older lady* didn't mean you didn't appreciate the male form in all its taut, firm and glistening glory. The cleaners were paid well with good company benefits and they did an excellent job. You might not believe it, but they genuinely did care for their older clientele and took pride in making sure they had clean homes to continue to live in safely.

Where were we?... Ah yes... Esme had been married to Bert for over sixty years. They had been very happy together with only the odd disagreement cropping up, such as whether curry sauce had a place on chips. Esme (quite correctly) argued it did not and produced evidence and witnesses to prove and win her case.

Three years ago, Bert died. Entirely his own fault after binge watching every episode of *Morecombe and Wise*; he'd laughed so much he had a heart attack and dropped dead on the floor. Although, the circumstances of his death were made worse in that he was up a ladder at the time of said heart attack changing a light bulb in the living room ceiling light, wearing his favourite 'onesie' given to him by a grandchild. Sadly, said garment was also highly flammable and at the very moment the heart attack struck there was a power surge from the light fitting which suddenly sparked, and as Bert fell from the ladder mid-heart attack the garment went up in flames. Luckily though, Esme was able to put the flames out quickly by drenching them in her freshly made bowl of tomato soup that she had just brought in.

Unluckily for Bert, his now sadly deceased body was covered in bright red tomato soup resembling a horror scene from a bad Halloween film. The vision certainly confused the paramedics when they arrived and tried to work out the cause of death just using the immediate visuals.

It wasn't all bad news though. Ultimately, Esme got her brand-new carpet she'd wanted for years, so not all was lost that night.

At 6.30p.m. every Tuesday, Esme's fifty-five-year-old son, Clive, dutifully drove round to his mother's house to take her to her weekly club. Esme had joined the local Women's Club after Bert died and Clive was happy to see that being in the club gave Esme a spring in her step and a new zest for life. Although, let's be honest, that could also have been Max the cleaner, but we won't tell Clive that.

Nothing stopped Esme from going to the weekly club or any of its regular outings. She loved it all.

"Evening, Mum," said Clive when Esme opened the front door.

"Hello, son," replied Esme.

"Off again?" asked Clive.

"Off again," replied Esme.

It was their ritual conversation each time Clive arrived each Tuesday. Just eight words but an entire conversation at that.

Clive waited for Esme to make her way to his car and opened the passenger door on her approach. He noticed she had started to use a walking stick of late but knew better than to ask her about it. When they were both strapped in and on their way to pick up Edith, Clive glanced at his mother and asked, "So, what's happening at the club tonight, Mum?"

A big smile appeared on Esme's face. "Tonight, son, we're having a talk and a demonstration."

"Oh really?" asked Clive. "What on?"

"Tea towels," said Esme with a triumphant tone. Clive pursed his lips together whilst trying to think of a suitable response. He couldn't think of one so just said, "Oh. Sounds, ummmm fascinating. Really… ummmm fascinating." Whilst internally thinking that if he ever got to an age where a talk on tea towels was a highlight of his week, he would make immediate plans to cease his own life forthwith.

It didn't take long to get to Edith's flat. She lived in a retirement complex for the over-sixties. At eighty-seven years old, Edith thought she'd be one of the oldest residents there, but she was pleased to find many people there in their nineties, the current oldest death dodger at ninety-eight so it meant a lot to her that she could say she was younger than most of her neighbours.

Edith was waiting outside for Clive; she knew he'd arrive dead on 6.45p.m. Clive liked to be punctual, precise and consistent. Edith thought him dull and boringly predictable, but she was happy to accept the lift to keep Esme company.

Clive pulled up right on time, leapt out and opened the rear passenger door and made sure Edith didn't bang her head whilst getting in. *Bless her*, thought Clive, *another fine older dependent lady with just a walker and a hearing aid but otherwise as fit as a fiddle.*

"HELLO, EDITH," Clive said loudly to make sure she could hear him. Edith looked up at him.

"What... what? What did you say?"

Clive smiled a sympathetic smile and repeated, "SORRY, EDITH – I SAID HELLO, EDITH."

"Oh," said Edith, "why didn't you say so to start with? Hello back to you, young Clive."

Esme shuffled round in her seat to (almost) face Edith, "EVENING, EDITH," she shouted.

Eventually when everyone was strapped in safely, Clive set off to the community centre. When they arrived, he could see it was going to be a busy evening in the club tonight; there must have been twenty or more old dears going in... *No*, thought Clive, *older persons*.

Clive parked as close as he could to the entrance and made sure that Esme and Edith got in OK. Goodbyes were said and he told them both he would be back at 8p.m. sharp to pick them up afterwards. As Clive drove off, he glanced in the rear-view mirror to see four more old dears, *older persons,* arrive.

Using his hands-free mobile in his car, he dialled his wife.

"Hi, Mary, just dropped them off, be back soon."

"You're an angel, Clive," said his wife. "What have they got on at the club tonight?"

"You'll never guess," replied Clive.

"Music from the war?" tried Mary. "Variety Hall music acts?"

"Nope," said Clive. "Tea towels."

"Sorry, Clive, you broke up there," said Mary. "Did you mean afternoon tea? Bit late though as it's almost 7p.m."

"No, Mary, tea towels. Actual tea towels." There was a pause before Mary could speak.

"Tea towels? As in the piece of material used to dry washed crockery? Tea? Towels?"

"You've got it. Actual tea towels!" said Clive as he drove off down the road.

"Bless," said Mary, stifling a giggle. "See you shortly."

Back in the hall when all the attendees had arrived, the club leader closed and locked the doors and drew the curtains. Edith removed her hearing aid and Esme chucked her walking stick on the floor next to her coat.

"So what did you tell him about tonight?" asked Edith.

"Tea towels," said Esme in a perfectly normal tone of voice.

"Bugger me," said Edith, "and the poor sap believed you?"

Esme smiled and nodded her head. "Oh yes."

"Bugger me," said Edith again.

One: part two

Edith Walker never married.

Not for the want of trying though.

Edith had been jilted at the altar three times, which many people would decry as bad luck and feel sorry for her. They'd feel less sorry though if they knew the more accurate truth, in that it was Edith who was the jilter and not the jilted.

First was Derek, a lovely man but with two MASSIVE front teeth. They'd never bothered Edith until the very moment she was walking up the aisle on her proud father's arm. As she and her father made that slow walk up the aisle together, Derek turned to see his blushing bride and just as he smiled, a ray of sunlight came through the stained-glass window lighting up his face and the huge smile he gave.

Edith didn't see the smile.

All Edith saw were the two MASSIVE front teeth now totally illuminated by the sun's rays and she suddenly felt her entire remaining life flash before her, realising that every day she would have to see *those* teeth. Remember, these were the days before NHS dentistry, so it was either pay for a back street butcher dentist to 'sort them out' or DIY dentistry. With each impending step up the aisle, Edith calculated the number of ways she could knock out those two front teeth and call it an accident. She wondered if there were any items that could be used as weapons in her bouquet that would do the job right now, if she accidently fell and hit Derek in the face with whichever implement she could find. Unlikely she calculated, getting ever closer to the altar and not seeing anything in the bouquet apart from flowers, ribbons and assorted green leaf. Could she really bear to spend even a few weeks of married life with 'the teeth' before a suitable implement and method came to her?

By the time Edith, still attached to proud father's arm, made it to the altar, she had made her decision.

The vicar standing at the altar began to intone…

"Dearly beloved, we are gathered here today to join this man and this woman in…"

"NO!" yelled Edith. "No, we're not!" before letting go of her confused father's arm and running back down the aisle quicker than the favourite in the 3.15 Queen Charlotte stakes at Epsom.

On the occasion of Edith's second attempt at a wedding, a smaller venue was procured, and a smaller wedding party gathered in joyful anticipation. This time, the (un)lucky groom was Jonathan Johnson, a slightly older man than her, Edith now being twenty-five and Jonathan thirty-nine.

The Johnson family were quite striking to look at, in the sense that all of them had a monobrow. Even the women. A thick black bushy monobrow. Honestly, it looked like someone had rolled together a long piece of charcoal, dipped it in glue, rolled it in the hair cuttings from a hairdressers and stuck it above the eyes.

Edith had always been perplexed by the female members of the clan's brows. How was it possible for both Jonathan Johnson's mother *and* father to have the same identical monobrow? Once again, with each step up the aisle, Edith focused on the offending facial hair. Had there been some sort of mucky jiggery pokery in the Johnsons' ancestors' past? Had their ancestors got a bit too overfamiliar with one another? What would happen if she and Jonathan Johnson had children? Would they all be cursed with the same offensive brow? Would she grow a sympathy brow once married? Edith shuddered as an image of her future daughter appeared in her mind and took her place at the altar staring back at Edith. Could Edith spend the rest of her life surrounded by brows from hell?

By the time Edith got to the top of the aisle, she had let go of her father's arm and as he stopped walking and remained in place at the altar, she carried on walking. Edith made a sharp left towards the fire exit and never saw Jonathan Johnson or his monobrow family ever again.

When it came to Edith's third attempt at exchanging marital vows, her father refused to a) pay for the wedding and b) walk her up the aisle. Edith's mother took to her bed with a fit of the vapours and refused to come out for the rest of the week.

Mr Walker still drove Edith to her wedding though, but he remained steadfast in his car with the engine running, expecting the inevitable.

He had made the right decision. Five minutes after the wedding started, the doors to the church flew open with gusto quickly followed by Edith running hell for leather, swiftly followed by the mother of the groom hurling flowers and profanities at her.

And that was the end of Edith's attempts to get married.

Edith decided to spare her parents' blushes and leave home for London. She packed her worldly goods into two small suitcases and set off for her future. She took rooms in a boarding house and accepted a job as a typist at the Ministry of Intelligence. It didn't take long for Edith and her bosses to realise she had a good head for figures and puzzles and without the shackles of a family, Edith's career blossomed, and the Security Services beckoned. If anyone ever asked, Edith would just say she was a typist and the most exciting thing she did all day was get the teas in for her boss and his visitors in between typing memos, filing correspondence and taking telephone calls.

Edith became accomplished in masking the truth and she realised that people always believed what she told them. It was a skill Edith realised she could use to her advantage. So often, the person you were talking to wasn't really interested at all in what you were saying so they'd only half listen. All you needed to do, was turn the conversation round so they'd end up talking about themselves and then *you* could quietly sit back and take it *all* in.

Edith also took to heart a lesson one of her section chiefs shared with her… whenever you were on a mission, it was best to carry out that mission in full sight of everyone. Because if you did it well, no one would take a blind bit of notice as to what you're really up to.

But as happens to us all, the ravages of time passed quickly and all too soon Edith found herself being pensioned off, albeit with a very handsome pension. Edith knew she could still make a difference and using her decades of knowledge from the Security Services, knew exactly which part of the country she was going to relocate to.

The village of Little Ormby in Norfolk was a hundred miles away from Edith's old life, but it had the right retirement home and the right club for her to join. The relocation went smoothly, and Edith settled in well. She made many friends in the home and whilst on regular trips to the village to get her shopping met Esme Smith. The two became firm friends and when Esme's husband died, Edith invited Esme to join her at the Women's Club.

Every Tuesday at 6.45p.m., Esme's son would arrive in his car with Esme to take them to the Women's Club. Nothing stopped them going; rain, wind, snow or ice, their attendance was sacrosanct. Clive was a nice boy, thought Edith (considering anyone under sixty-five to be a child). Nice but dull. Very dull. Duller than a dull day in Dulwich. Clive, ever the gentleman, leapt out of his car and opened the rear passenger door for her.

"HELLO, EDITH," Clive said loudly to make sure she could hear him. Edith looked up at him.

"What… what? What did you say?"

Clive smiled a sympathetic smile and repeated, "SORRY EDITH, I SAID HELLO."

"Oh," said Edith, "why didn't you say so to start

with? Hello back to you, Clive." Esme shuffled round in her seat to (almost) face Edith, "EVENING, EDITH," she shouted.

Eventually when everyone was strapped in safely, Clive set off to the community centre. When they arrived, he could see it was going to be a busy evening in the club tonight; there must have been twenty or more old dears going in... *No*, thought Clive, *older persons*.

Clive parked as close as he could to the doors and made sure that Esme and Edith got in OK. Goodbyes were said and he told them both he would be back at 8p.m. sharp to pick them up afterwards.

Back in the hall when all of the attendees had arrived, the club leader closed and locked the doors and drew the curtains.

Edith removed her hearing aid and Esme chucked her walking stick on the floor next to her coat.

"So what did you tell him about tonight?" asked Edith.

"Tea towels," said Esme in a perfectly normal tone of voice.

"Bugger me," said Edith, "and the poor sap believed you?"

Esme smiled and nodded her head. "Oh yes."

"Bugger me," said Edith again.

One: part three

Doris

Back in the hall when all the attendees had arrived, the club president, Marjory Bartlett, closed and locked the doors then pulled the curtains to.

Marjory dimmed the hall lights and drew back the stage curtain to reveal a very large display screen. The screen flickered and buzzed a bit until she kicked it to bring it back into life. Two women appeared, one on either side of the screen. The woman on the left, was in a millinery workshop surrounded by wooden hat blocks and the woman on the right, in a bakery surrounded by baking tins.

"Good evening, ladies," the two women on screen said in unison. The audience, as one, replied back.

"Good evening, Delores," looking at the lady on the left.

"Good evening, Agnes," looking at the lady on the right.

Delores was Delores Marshall, milliner owner and proprietor of Hats with Attitude, Agnes was Agnes Trevin, baker owner and proprietor of Bring on the Cake.

"Thank you for coming along tonight," said Delores.

"Complimentary tea towels will be given out at the end to ensure cover is maintained."

"The new regional police centre in Wymondham is having an open day at the end of the month," said Agnes, "and we've arranged for you to cater at the event in your role as local ambassadors and in exchange for your time and effort, the force has agreed to give you a behind-the-scenes tour of the new premises."

"We need for you to locate and take copies of all the information they have in any files they have marked 'Armadillo' and photograph all the evidence they have collected. Once you have finished your mission in the field, we need you to get the copies back to us as soon as possible," said Delores.

"'Armadillo' is part of a long-running case we're working on," said Agnes. "We'll likely revisit it many times over the coming months, but right now we need to know what the police think they know and what they think is evidence. We'll then be getting the Cornwall group to do the same, followed by Edinburgh."

"We couldn't do this without you," said Delores. "After all, who'd suspect the redoubtable Women's Club as one of, if not, *the* finest underground intelligence-gathering agency of all time." The Women's Club members all nodded their heads in absolute agreement of her assessment.

"All of the details are in the tea towels," continued Delores. "I made them myself—"

"Only because you wouldn't let me help you," interjected Agnes.

"Because, Agnes dear, you wanted to staple the edges together. Who on earth has a tea towel with stapled edges?

It would not only scratch whatever you're meant to be frying…"

"Frying?" asked Agnes.

"Drying," said Delores. "It would also arouse suspicion which we need to avoid at all costs."

"Well, if you insist," said Agnes, whose faith in staples overrode what little, well, no talent she had for sewing.

"Ladies, just run a warm iron over the towels and the full mission statement on Armadillo will appear," said Delores. "You'll understand why we need the copies. Once you're fully up to speed, wash the tea towels at 60 degrees and the wording will disappear. They can then be used normally or kept to maintain the illusion of a commemorative tea towel. In the meantime, we have every faith in you and your mission abilities."

"We'll leave the finer distract and copy details up to you and reconvene in a few weeks' time for a progress report. Until then, the Millinery Bakers Detective Agency thanks you for your service," said Agnes.

"Over and out," said Delores removing her and Agnes from the online meeting, but not before the audience saw (as the screen faded) Agnes turn to her right, as if looking at Delores on the screen, and say, "Well, I still think staples are a sound idea."

"Idiot," was Delores's simple and succinct retort as the screen faded to black and the live feed ended.

The rest of the Women's Club meeting was taken up in the planning of how they would distract the police to give them the time and secure space needed to access the files.

Edith suggested they ran a 'Billy'.

Esme offered a 'Tank in Two Acts'.

Pat went with a 'Tea and Biscuits'. A strong contender considering they would be there to cater at the police event.

Marjory pulled the group back in with a Triple Doris. This gave cause for the group to all make noises of agreement and vigorously nod their heads (although this did make Janica Webb's blue rinse tight perm wig fall back a little, but no one said anything as she pulled it back up, even if was ever so slightly wonky).

The Triple Doris would open with Doris suddenly announcing she felt faint as she had forgotten to take her medication. Doris would fall to the ground banging her head, causing panic in the force with those in the room rushing to the eighty-one-year-old's aid. For the record, Doris was a professional faller, having worked in the circus all her life. She could fall from low or great heights for dramatic effect and walk away unharmed, but the police didn't need to know this.

The middle act of the Triple Doris would be Doris announcing she had lost her hearing aid. There would be much shouting as she would now be completely deaf,[1] and there would be dramatic wails as she and the group started rifling through papers (in plain and obvious sight of the coppers) trying to find it. The sight and sound of a rampaging tribe of OAPs could be quite terrifying so again no one would notice a couple of the ladies taking the odd photo and downloading a few files from a nearby unsecured computer.

The finale of the Triple Doris would be Doris

---

[1] not true

announcing in a very loud and urgent voice that she needed the toilet. She would need the toilet *right there and then* and would go into detail if needed. No one, *really* no one, would want to hear the exact nature of the toiletage required, especially when followed up with urgent cries of 'it's coming' or 'I can't stop dripping'. The other ladies would then come in with 'has anyone got a spare pad?' which was guaranteed to make most people recoil, especially when a swarm of pads would then be hoisted aloft from the numerous handbags the Women's Club members would have brought in with them. Once more, in the melee, no one would notice a few photographs being taken and the odd document copied.

The group made one further amendment to the Triple Doris, which was to follow it up with the 'Where's Doris?' if they needed more time. In this situation, upon coming to the end of their HQ tour and tea duty visit they would announce that Doris was missing. There would be much commotion as the fear and panic spread that one of the old ladies had disappeared. The ladies would then fan out in a pincer movement in all directions moving at speed to find their missing friend. The coppers wouldn't know who to follow first as the ladies would outnumber them and move with a surprising sudden agility and speed.

No one in the group was called Doris. Each Doris would be played by a different lady. No one would realise that all the Dorises were different. All that would be seen was a group of frail old ladies who brought cake and biscuits with them for the open day. One of them was bound to be called Doris would be the assumption. After all, that's what old ladies are called.

Age and assumptions were the two best attributes at the Women's Club intelligence gatherings. It is oft said that when women age, they become invisible, and the rest of the world forgets they are there. But, as the members of the Women's Club would also tell you, *this* is the greatest advantage of them all, as chatter becomes loose, secrets become shared and plans become known.

Those loose lips never cotton on that their plans are being recorded, catalogued and reported back to central command. And never in a million years, in a million line-ups would anyone pick out the hunchbacked little old lady with a purple rinse, hearing aid and a walker as the secret agent.

Esme, Edith, Marjory, Pat and all the other members of the Women's Club knew they were the lucky ones. There were many older people whose bodies, minds or both may have let them down in older age leaving them less able to live their lives as they once did. But for as long as they could, they and all the other nationwide Women's Club members would continue to amass intelligence for the Millinery Bakers Detective Agency and woe betide *anyone* who got in their way.

One: part four

Clive

Clive got to the hall about ten minutes before the meeting ended. He liked to be early so he could pull up close, so his mum and Edith didn't have far to walk.

He glanced out of the side window to see Marjory Bartlett open the hall curtains so he knew the ladies would be out soon. He turned off the radio and leapt out of the driver's seat to open the rear door behind him before swiftly moving to the front of the car to open the front passenger door. The hall doors opened, and the club members began to shuffle out, each of them proudly clutching a tea towel, which seemed to be embroidered with the words 'Little Ormby'.

"Sad," he said to himself. "What a way to end up."

Clive never saw Esme and Edith roll their eyes at him as he got back into his driver's seat once they were safely strapped in. Clive never saw the knowing looks the club members shared as they were collected by their respective family members.

Poor Clive.

Heart of gold.

Brain the size of a pea.

One: part five

Delores

Delores Marshall was a talented milliner with a fine reputation. She apprenticed with some of the best milliners in London and France and was even tutored by milliners to the royal family. Discretion and diplomacy of course forbid from detailing whom.

Hats with Attitude had customers nationwide and you name it, Delores made it. Weddings, christenings, racing, society events, ladies' pieces, menswear and children's headwear to boot. Hell yes, Delores even had a funeral range… it was a surprising growing market. There was no end to the list of events that people wanted a headpiece for.

Bespoke, custom made to measure or choose a piece from the 'ready to wear' range, available to buy or hire, Delores had got your headwear covered.

In her spare time, Delores liked to give talks and demonstrations to community groups, craft fairs, schools and colleges. It helped to keep heritage crafts alive, and Delores always hoped to find someone as enthusiastic and passionate about millinery as her, so she could offer an apprenticeship and give someone the same opportunity that she had.

On top of this, Delores also competed in national and international millinery competitions. Sometimes she did well and sometimes not so well but every competition brought new skills, new ways of creative thinking, new ways of working and lots of new people to meet. The competitions could also bring intrigue and deception with a hint of potential corruption and bribery but that's a story for another time.

Hats with Attitude was Delores's passion. Nothing made her happier than designing and creating that perfect piece for her client. With fingers and hands the colour of Golden Yellow or Emerald Green, the same shade as the feathers she was dying, or when stabbing her fingers with hat pins and sewing needles to the point where she could no longer feel the pain, this is what Delores did best, and she knew it was entirely worth it when the finished piece was handed over to her client and she saw the look of joy and pure happiness looking back at her.

In 2020, when the global pandemic hit, the events that brought Delores her business stopped. Not a gradual stop but a sudden and full-blown immediate whack-you-in-the-face (whilst wearing a face mask) stop. Delores could no longer rely on her millinery business to pay the bills. She needed to find another source of income and quickly.

Having thought about it for precisely thirty-seven seconds she knew that Agnes (owner of Bring on the Cake) seemed to have a knack for finding people and tracking their entire life based on their social media accounts. If they could combine Agnes's technical skills and her own people skills then maybe, just maybe, they could form a sideline business which might just get them through the strange Covid days.

Delores was known to be a 'people person'. She loved to talk to people and get to know them. She made them feel relaxed and comfortable and happy to chat to her. Many of her clients returned, many brought friends, and many found it their only opportunity to relax and unwind.

Delores also realised that some clients wanted to speak freely but couldn't always as they were 'accompanied' by someone else. So, she created a safe space at the back of the workshop calling it a 'changing room' where clients could get dressed in their special outfit and try on their headpiece in private to make sure it was a perfect fit. What no one else knew, apart from Delores and her client, was that the room was soundproof and locked on the inside so *no one* on the outside could hear or get in. With a potential idea for a new business venture for her and Agnes, Delores knew that once life had returned to something a bit more normal, this space could be used to meet those in need of a new service. Until then, they'd have to meet in the virtual world.

On that fateful day in April 2020, Delores went out for her one-hour government-sanctioned walk and saw Agnes coming towards her. Maintaining the legal-two metre distance, Delores said to Agnes…

"I've got an idea."

One: part six

Agnes

Agnes Trevin was a baker who did everything from cakes to biscuits to breads. It was never meant to be her full-time job – Agnes had lived and worked in London for many years and for a long time enjoyed her job. But, following an aggressive takeover, the job itself became less enjoyable and the old team who were more like family, was replaced with a new guard who were in it only for themselves. It's quite normal for someone not to enjoy their job but they survive each day when surrounded by a great team. Once those people are swapped out for less pleasant colleagues then it's lose lose.

Fortunately for Agnes, she had some luck when a distant cousin died and left their entire estate to Agnes. Obviously, this was not so lucky for the cousin who was now dead, but it was for Agnes who ended up with a very nice inheritance. It wasn't enough money to retire on and live a millionaire lifestyle, but it enabled Agnes to leave her job, sell her London flat and do something that she had always wanted to do.

Bake.

Agnes moved back to Norfolk where she grew up and set up Bring on the Cake in a small retail complex in Little Ormby, a medium-sized village directly on the mid-Norfolk coast which had a good mix of permanent residents and seasonal holiday trade.

It didn't take long for the business to take off. The offering was good-quality products, always baked freshly at sensible prices. Events could be catered for with bespoke cookies or cupcakes, and local businesses supplied with cakes and biscuits for their morning and afternoon tea breaks.

In 2020, when the global pandemic hit, the everyday trade that brought Agnes her business stopped. It was a gradual stop though as food retailers were considered essential business. To start with, Agnes was okay as whilst the business and holidaymaker trade had stopped, the everyday walk-ins continued to come. Well, they formed a two-metre gapped queue outside. The problem though was the rapidly growing unavailability of ingredients.

The price of flour rocketed as supply ran short when the panic buying started. Once supermarkets ran out of stock, people started buying direct from wholesalers who were desperate to shift their stock but at top-dollar prices. Agnes tried to keep going as best as she could. Bedecked in a face mask and hazmat suit, she started baking and giving away bread to as many locals as she could to keep them fed, but the time came when even this had to come to an end with a full-blown stop to operations.

Having thought about it for precisely thirty-seven seconds she knew that Delores (owner of Hats with

Attitude) always seemed to have a knack for finding people who needed help. If they could combine Delores's people skills and Agnes's own skills at tracking down certain information online then maybe, just maybe, they could form a sideline business which might just get them through the strange Covid days.

She knew that Delores had a secure room which could possibly be used to meet potential clients, although until the restrictions eased this would have to be a longer-term option. In the meantime, she could set up a secure web-based meeting portal and connect those in need digitally.

Agnes also decided that when life was back to normal, she could continue to supply tea and biscuits to Hats with Attitude. After all, cups and plates meant fingerprints and she knew that Delores got absolutely everyone to try on the headpieces in the showroom, and headpieces which pull out a hair or two = DNA.

On that fateful day in April 2020, Agnes went out for her one-hour government-sanctioned walk and saw Delores coming towards her. Maintaining the legal two-metre distance, Agnes said to Delores…

"I've got an idea."

Two

Wednesday, 1st December 2021

The actual first calendar day of December seemed a long way off in coming. Thoughts of December seemed to begin way back in July when shops started sneaking in tubs of festive chocolates. Throughout the land, everyone wondered whether it was new stock or last year's unsold fare. Either way, the number of shoppers who ended up with a tub or two in their trolley vastly exceeded the number of shoppers who didn't, which meant the supermarkets were entirely justified in saying the only reason they put Christmas stuff out in mid-July was because customers bought the products. The supermarket customers still complained and still disputed this reasoning, without the faintest concept of irony as they still picked up another selection box in July and then some tinsel in August. Then tree lights, wrapping paper and boxes of baubles in October along with their Halloween sweets and scary costumes.

But eventually the months on the calendar gave way and the page finally turned to December.

In Little Ormby, the buzz and chaos of the summer holidaymakers now seemed a long time ago and a long time away until the next season. But seasonal events in line with any Covid restrictions were still taking place for the locals. The village Christmas lights had been switched on just the week before and there was to be a lantern parade with carols along the beach (weather permitting) and on into the village centre at the weekend. It always had a good turnout and everyone had been sad when the event couldn't run the previous December, so turnout was expected to be big, if still socially distanced.

For Delores, this was a quieter time of the year when it came to customer orders, but December was when she carried out her annual stock take, when she got the books ready for the accountant and when she began and finished the workshop tidy and clean. There were still a few unexpected clients who'd been invited to a last minute event where they'd need to dress up and the diary was full of clients, new and old, with consultations starting mid-January onwards for the 2022 social events. Then there were demonstrations to go to, exhibitions to enter and talks to various groups taking up a huge chunk of the diary already. Delores loved to share her passion with other people and when she got asked to attend such events she said yes, yes, yes! The only time she maybe regretted this was when she looked at the orders piling up with clients arriving in just a few days to collect their bespoke pieces which she hadn't had time to start, let alone finish. But Delores never let anyone down; she'd work through the night if needed, waking up only when her head fell on a hat block which led to some interesting-shaped bruises.

There was also many a time when she'd woken up with a bewildering range of feathers in her hair. She sometimes looked like a new species of feathered bird which was only found on the Norfolk coast.

Delores also spent time putting the finishing touches to the Spring/Summer 2022 collection; the display pieces were pretty much done but there was always one supplier who delivered late or feathers that refused to take the colour she was trying to dye them. It was also time to start thinking about Autumn/Winter 2022/3; things had to be planned that far in advance to stay on trend. Delores carried with her a notebook (she called it *The Book*). Whenever inspiration struck, Delores would note down the thoughts in *The Book* and refer to them when it was time to start creating the vision.

With a deep breath, Delores knew she couldn't put off the inevitable. It was time for the winter workshop tidy. Putting on her favourite high-power tunes she rocked and bopped, and power-sang her way through six hours of tidying up.

The end result was very pleasing. All the rolls of material back in the racks, sorted by colour and shade from light to dark. The many, many pairs of scissors hanging back on the board from the smallest in size to the largest, all sharpened to a fine edge. Hat block pins sorted by shape and colour and placed neatly back into their storage tubs. Petersham ribbons, wires, beads and crystals, glue, feathers, sinamay, silk, combs, velvets, bias binding you name it, they were all sorted, catalogued and put away. The workshop looked incredible and could have been photographed for a magazine.

The problem though was that Delores didn't have anything to hand anymore on her workbench. She had to spend time (although she would describe this as 'waste time') retrieving what she needed, so by approximately 10.36a.m. on the 2nd of January the workshop would be back to how it looked before the annual tidy.

This caused Agnes much internal discombobulation; she believed in neat and tidy, a place for everything and everything in its place. Delores told her that she agreed entirely with this sentiment. However, *the place* where everything in 'its place' was, was on her bench right where she actually needed it.

"It's neither organised nor disorganised," she said to Agnes, "it's Delorganised."

Agnes's December and Christmas began in detail almost one year to the day from the previous Christmas and even then, it was usually the previous year's Halloween when she began to at least outline the plan for the following year's Christmas. There were orders to place with suppliers for delivery early May to ensure that, come June, the mincemeat could be made and turned every four weeks until needed. Christmas puddings needed to be made in June and July (and nothing says Christmas more than making and steaming 1,000 Christmas puddings in a 34-degree three-week heatwave in summer). Christmas cakes to be made by the 31st of October, duly fed with alcohol then covered in marzipan and iced in December.

Icing was not a strong point for Agnes. She had no problem baking and could turn out anything, but when it came to icing, and especially delicate decorative piping, she turned into a stark-raving-mad screaming banshee.

The hysteria peaked with icing ending up on Agnes, the floor, every work surface available, the fridge door and still unclear as to how, but on the back door windowpane as well. Agnes could ruin hours of baking perfection in just forty-six seconds if given a piping bag and a nozzle. She'd been on courses and had someone come in for one-to-one training, but every course was failed, and the one-to-one tutor left very quickly with icing in their hair and a number nine nozzle protruding from an ear.

One year, Agnes came across a new ready-to-roll icing, which was called Silver Sparkle and had a very pretty picture on the front. Agnes had no problem rolling out and applying marzipan to a cake so she decided there was no reason why she couldn't do ready-to-roll icing. In theory, she was right, it rolled evenly and was very simple to place on the cake. It was just a shame that the colour in reality was not Silver Sparke but Freshly Laid Tarmac Grey.

Suffice to say, if you ordered a Christmas cake from Agnes and you wanted Agnes to ice it, the end result would be rough iced blobs representing snowy peaks and snow drifts and lots and lots of decorations on the top. It should be pointed out though, that for special occasion cakes, Agnes hired an actual cake-decorating professional who always did a beautiful job and never once iced the back door in anger. A win-win situation.

For Christmas 2021, Agnes was also doing a fine trade in Christmas Bauble Swiss Rolls. They could be made, filled and frozen in advance and then just brought out and finished when needed. Even Agnes could blob little swirls of buttercream on the top and shove a chocolate tree, a reindeer and a Santa in each buttercream blob. Like Delores, there was also the year-end stock take to conduct. Agnes was pleased the dried fruits could be done by weight and not individually. "Life is too short to count sultanas," she told herself.

This year, Agnes had also started to offer a Twelfth Night cake. It seemed to be growing in popularity as people tried to keep the festive spirit alive for the whole twelve days of Christmas, instead of getting bored and fed up with it all by 6p.m. on Boxing Day.

You'd think everyone would be sick of fruit cake after getting through an entire Christmas cake in just a few days, but as it turned out, there is always room for cake.

The final feast of Christmas (Twelfth Night) was marked by the taking down of the decorations, a celebratory evening feast and the consumption of a special cake. A bit like a Christmas pudding which would have a coin baked in it to bring whoever found it good luck and good fortune for the following year (providing of course they hadn't choked to death on the coin), a Twelfth Night cake had a dried butterbean baked in it. Whoever found the butterbean was declared King or Queen Bean. Historically a Twelfth Night cake would have been very elaborate in its intricate decor to show off the wealth of the family, but the words 'Agnes', 'elaborate', 'intricate' and 'decor' were not words that went together so Agnes rough-iced her cakes and on top of each one, placed a crown made of sugar paste to represent the bean monarch.

Christmas for Agnes was one of the busiest times of the year and financially critical so as she also muttered to herself on more than one occasion… "Bring on the cake!"

As it turned out, December also brought with it an intriguing case for the Millinery Bakers Detective Agency and as usual, it all started with Delores.

Three

Thursday, 2nd December 2021

Thursday, 2nd December dawned bright and cold but heralded the ending of the second national lockdown. It had been a chilly night, down to just 5 degrees but it felt much colder, as if there should have been a sharp frost or snow on the ground making everywhere look like a wintery Christmas card scene. Delores shivered as she opened the workshop doors; she was looking forward to getting the heating on and her morning wake-up cup of coffee. She limited herself to just one cup of coffee a day as any more than that and the caffeine would go straight to her head meaning she couldn't be trusted to walk a straight line, let alone sew one.

With the workshop starting to warm up, Delores looked at the diary to see what was on for today. She was expecting a delivery from Fabric Kings at some point, her new hat block from Best on the Block, but just two clients today. That morning, Audrey Wilkins would dial in for her monthly virtual visit. Audrey never bought anything, she just admired the collections on display and enjoyed talking to Delores. For her part, Delores knew that Audrey was lonely, and this was one of the few occasions she got to spend in the company of someone else, so she was happy to give her the time, and before Covid, a warm place to sit and a hot drink for an hour or two.

Later that afternoon, Ellen Crispin was due; she was booked in for 2p.m. Ellen was a good customer; she was the finance director of Crispin Crisps, a major employer in Norfolk. Ellen was married to the current MD, Charles Crispin (the third generation Crispin to run the family business). Ellen attended many events, locally and nationally, and always wore a bespoke Delores Marshall, Hats with Attitude headpiece. Looking ahead to mid-2022 onwards, Ellen had already accepted invitations to three christenings, six weddings, five trade conferences with posh evening dinners and she was pretty sure there would be at least three funerals before June, so she had to plan outfits in advance.

Spot on 2p.m., the workshop door opened, and the bell jingled to announce Ellen's arrival. Pleasantries of the season were exchanged, and hot drinks made before Ellen and Delores retired to the comfy chairs (but sitting a good two metres apart) to go through the next season's looks, styles and design options.

Ellen brought sample swatches of the outfits she had planned so Delores could match the headpiece colours and she also brought in drawings of each outfit. Most of the outfits were being custom made and were not yet ready as completed items so Delores wouldn't get to see Ellen in the outfit until later, but she knew Ellen's style well enough by now to mentally envisage the final vision and so she could talk through options. Ellen also brought with her a selection box of forty-eight Crispin Christmas Crisps ranging in flavour from Roast Turkey (*very nice*, thought Delores) to Mince Pies and Cream (*give to Agnes,* thought Delores).

The consultation took a good few hours, but Delores noticed that Ellen didn't seem her usual self. The enthusiasm was lacking. She said all the right words of course but the smile wasn't genuine and quite often Ellen would stare into the distance until Delores could reign her back in. Delores made Ellen another hot drink and when she brought it over to where they were sitting, Delores asked Ellen if she was all right.

"Ellen, are you OK? You seem preoccupied, like you need to be somewhere else. We can always finish this off another time if you need?" Ellen looked down at her feet then back to Delores.

"Truth is, Delores, that I just don't know what to do… Something terrible has happened at the factory and..." Ellen paused, looked away and took a deep breath before continuing, "I'm just so lost, I'm going round in circles trying to work out what's best. It's all I've been able to think about, but Charles won't take it seriously and any time I try to talk to him about it, he just shouts back and storms off. We even had to call the Yarmouth police and they took some details but said there was very little to go on and pretty much left us to it. Charles says that puts an end to it, but I just can't stop thinking about it. What if something really bad happens next and I did nothing to stop it? I just… I just don't know anymore what to do for the best."

Delores closed the consultation book and sighed.

"Ellen, you know that myself and Agnes from Bring on the Cake, run a detective agency on the side?"

Ellen nodded her head. Delores continued, "Would you like us to help and see what we can do? We can be discreet and we're not the police so surely Charles wouldn't mind?"

Ellen crumpled with relief and nodded her head again.

"Yes, oh yes please, that would be such a relief. Even if you tell me at the end that I'm the crazy one, at least I know I'll have done something. I just can't go on like this."

Delores sat up straight and stretched out her arms and fingers (she never realised she did this every time a case was afoot, but it was a hundred percent her tell). "Are you okay to stay on a bit longer, Ellen? I'll need to get hold of Agnes to see if she's free to pop round so we can formally get all the details and make a start for you."

"I can stay until 6ish but then need to be back at the house as we've got guests tonight."

"Perfect," said Delores, texting Agnes. "Whilst we're waiting for Agnes to reply, can you give me some headlines as to what's happened at the factory?"

There was a pause, Ellen looked away into the distance again then back at Delores.

"I think someone is trying to destroy the business. Staff have been poisoned, or had cruel jokes played on them, nasty emails have been sent, machinery has been tampered with, orders cancelled with suppliers and tyres slashed on lorries. It's just been awful."

"Well I'm not surprised you're so worried, Ellen, I'd be too if that was my business," said Delores.

"But that's not the worst thing though," replied Ellen.

"What could be worse than that?" asked Delores.

"I think it's our son who's doing it."

Delores's surprise at Ellen's revelation was only broken by the sudden hammering of the workshop door. Both women jumped and turned to see a dishevelled-looking Agnes gesturing to be let in.

As Delores unlocked and opened the door, she said to Agnes, "I know you like gardening but why do you look like you've been dragged backwards through a hedge? Oh dear Lord please don't tell me you've *actually* been dragged through a hedge backwards."

"Nope," panted Agnes, "vindictive duvet cover." Taking a deep intake of breath, Agnes let forth in one go. "It's my day off so I decided to change the bedding but I still can't understand how a duvet and a duvet cover which have four corners each and which should line up when changed multiply by sixty-four and I end up with more corners than actual corners and then duvet lumps and bumps in all directions, then the only way to fix it is to get in between the duvet and the cover and then it tries to eat you and none of the corners still line up so you give up and then the phone rings and you have to get out of the duvet sandwich but you can't because of all the corners and then you have a bit of a panic attack because you're trapped so you have to fight your way out and now here I am."

"Do you feel better now you've got that off your chest?" asked Delores.

"Yes, thank you," said Agnes flattening down her wild hair and pulling up a chair whilst choosing to sit two metres away from both Ellen and Delores. "Hello, Ellen, I hear you need our help."

Ellen looked up at Agnes. "Hello, Agnes, yes, I really think I do," said Ellen. "Maybe it would be best if I started at the beginning."

"That's usually the best place to start," said Delores.

"Do you mind if I record this?" asked Agnes whipping out a Dictaphone from her ridiculously small handbag.

"That's fine, go ahead," replied Ellen to Agnes. Ellen took a breath then a sip of tea and began at the beginning.

"What do you both know about Crispin Crisps?"

Delores replied, "It's been here for as long as I can remember."

Agnes agreed. "Same here. I know the factory was very well established decades before I moved to Norfolk."

"The factory was founded by my husband's grandfather, the first Charles Crispin, and he opened the factory in 1950. He had a very clear vision of what he wanted to do: use local produce from local farmers and employ local workers. He wanted to make a good-quality crisp, but one that was available to everyone." Ellen paused for a sip of tea before continuing. "At that time it was just single bags and plain so no flavours, not even salted. Charles I retired in 1965, actually aged sixty-five and when he retired, his son Charles II took over. You'll see a pattern; all the first-born sons are called Charles. Anyway, Charles II – my husband's father – was only thirty-five when he took on the business; young but very successful. He grew the business, introduced flavours, increased production, employed more locals, but he still retained those original values that his father insisted on. Local products, local farmers, local workers. He did really well before retiring in 1995, also at sixty-five. That meant my husband took over, Charles III. He was forty so a little bit older than his father was when he took over the business." Ellen paused again and took another sip of tea and crunched a 'Ready Salted Crunch Crisp' crisp. "Like his father and his grandfather before him, my Charles still holds onto those original values. But he was still able to grow the business, launching healthier products (baked and not fried). He even introduced seasonal flavours such as Mince Pie and Cream for Christmas and an Easter Marzipan crisp."

"Marzipan flavour?" said Delores, looking a little bit horrified.

"I don't remember that one," said Agnes.

"It didn't sell well," said Ellen. "To be honest they weren't my favourite either, but when you hear of some of the flavours that companies launch now maybe we were just ahead of our time. Anyway, speaking of time, my husband has no plans to retire. Something that causes our son, Charles IV, a great deal of frustration. We have two children by the way: Charles IV, who we call Charlie, and Lizzie, our daughter. Both work within the business."

"I'm still fixated on a Marzipan flavour crisp," said Delores. "It was *definitely* an unusual crisp flavour. Sorry, Ellen, carry on."

"The management is made up of Charles as MD, I'm Financial Director then our son is General Director and heir to the business, Lizzie is Supply Chain Director and Charles's younger brother Crispin is Brand and Marketing Director. Charles's sister, Karen, used to be on the board, but she resigned when her and her husband emigrated to Australia a few years back to try and set up a Crispin Crisps factory over there. It didn't work out, but they decided to stay there and make new lives for themselves in the sunshine."

Agnes and Delores looked at one another, then back at Ellen. They both looked bemused.

"Crispin Crispin?" asked Delores.

"Yes, Crispin Crispin," said Ellen. "I'm afraid their parents had a sense of humour failure on that one. He's always hated his name so goes by CC instead."

"Well, I'm not surprised," said Agnes. "I would too."

Ellen continued, "We also have Malcolm Carson as New Product Director, Jayne Johns as Legal Director, Richard Coates as HR Director and finally Anne Mayhew, PA to Charles. We think the management board is a good mix of family and non-family to get the balance right."

"You said your son Charlie is next in line to take over the business, but he's already older than your Charles was when he took on the business. Is that why you think he's responsible?" asked Delores.

"He's been very vocal about the way the business is run and all the changes he wants to make, and he's never denied being responsible for all the unpleasant events of this year. But equally we've, well I've never been able to prove anything. I hope it's not him. I really hope it's not him, but I just don't know," replied Ellen shrugging her shoulders.

"Well, that's where we can help you," said Agnes, "but are you sure you really want us to look into this for you? If we find out it is Charlie who's responsible, you won't be able to unhear it or take it back. The truth might be what you don't want to hear so the consequences of finding out can't be ignored."

Ellen nodded. "I know… Delores said the same thing earlier, but enough's enough. I need to take control of this and find out once and for all. For me, for the family and for the business."

"Okay," said Agnes, "if you're sure, then we'll be happy to help. We'll need to take some more details and I'll get some forms for you to fill out, but for now can you give us a bit more detail of the events?"

Ellen nodded, took a breath and began. "It started back in January, well, late January really. We'd got through the awful year of 2020 which I thought was bad enough, but I thought 2021 would be better. As a food manufacturer we stayed open throughout the lockdowns, but insisted any office-based staff who wanted to work from home could. Then for factory-based staff we changed the shift patterns – we went for more shifts but shorter working patterns so we could have fewer people working to keep the numbers low. It meant we could still produce the same number of crisps but over longer hours with fewer staff on the shop floor to keep them safe but without impacting their pay. We got in all the PPE, the free Covid tests, we came up with contingency plans when there was an outbreak and supported everyone whose home life was disrupted. We did everything we could in such an awful year."

Agnes and Delores nodded, agreeing entirely with what Ellen was telling them about the changes which had to be made to keep a business running. They had themselves both faced challenges keeping their respective businesses afloat and even now still faced disruptions.

Ellen continued. "Well I thought nothing could be worse than 2020 but then January 2021 came along. As well as still working within the current restrictions, I got a phone call from our business manager at the bank who manages our account. He wanted more information on our current finances in relation to a business loan we were looking at taking for some machinery upgrades. He wanted clarification on the email sent to him which confirmed we'd massively adjusted our next financial year's trading performance forecast downwards and that we wouldn't be able to make the repayments we'd previously agreed. He wanted to see the exact forecast reduction, know the reasons for the reductions and what plans we had in place to mitigate."

"There were so many businesses that went under last year," said Agnes. "You did so well to stay afloat but with the ongoing restrictions I'm not surprised you had to reduce your forecast."

"But that's the problem," said Ellen, "we didn't reduce our forecast and we didn't dispute our planned monthly loan payments."

"I take it the email was fake?" asked Delores.

"Completely and utterly fake. The bank forwarded it back to me, and I'd certainly never seen it before. None of the claims it made were true. The person who sent it doesn't even exist, but the damage was done."

"Did the email come from inside the company?" asked Agnes.

"It did, yes," said Ellen. "Our IT department checked it out and it came from our server, but how… they don't know."

"So someone got access to your system, was able to create an email account and send an email from inside the company?" questioned Agnes. "That's a majorly serious security breach."

"I agree," said Ellen, "but no one knows how."

Agnes looked puzzled and somewhat disbelieving. Delores looked at Ellen and said, "I don't understand how someone external to your business can access your systems. It would be like Agnes remotely accessing my business laptop and being able to view my records."

Agnes looked at Delores. "Been there. Done that," she said, then asked Ellen quickly. "What happened next?" before Delores could react.

Ellen continued. "I sat down with the business manager, showed him all the ledgers, all the transactions in and out, every penny. I gave him the benefits (financially speaking) the new machinery would bring to our production and sales... everything. It took a lot of time and effort to get him back onside. But understandably the bank wasn't impressed that someone unknown had accessed the system, and it really knocked their trust in us. I managed to get them back onside, but it's been an uneasy relationship ever since."

"If it wasn't an outside hacker then it has to be someone on the inside. Would Charlie have access to set up an email address and send an email to the bank?" asked Delores.

"Access, yes, but he's never been particularly into the IT side of things, so I don't know how he'd know or be able to create an account," said Ellen.

"Well, not unless someone from your IT team helped him," said Agnes. "I take it you confronted him about this?"

Ellen nodded her head in agreement. "He just laughed it off. Kept saying 'oh, what a shame, who on earth could have had a reason for doing that?'. Charles brushed it off as well when I tried speaking to him about it. He said it was all sorted now, so time to move on."

"But it wasn't sorted?" asked Delores.

"No. A few weeks later, must have been around mid-February, I got another call, this time from a finance journalist from the *Norfolk County* newspaper. She'd received an email from someone at the factory detailing we were in trouble and that the banks had been notified. She wanted to know if we were at risk of closing, and if everyone would lose their jobs."

"Was it from the same person as before?" asked Agnes.

"No, it was from a different person (who also doesn't exist) but still with a company email address and again sent from our servers."

"So it still could have been the same person but using a different email address?" said Agnes.

"Possibly," said Ellen, "but we got the journalist in, had a chat and showed her the books like we did with the bank. She went away happy; well, not happy that her time had been wasted but happy we were going to survive as a business."

"She didn't want to look into the fact that someone unknown was accessing your internal systems?" asked Agnes.

"No, not when she realised she'd been sent a hoax mail. She put it down to a disgruntled employee and it wasn't worth her time for a non-story."

"And did you ask Charlie about this one as well?" asked Agnes.

"I did. And like before, he just laughed, and Charles wouldn't take it further. But it left me unsettled again and I was totally on edge. Anyway, it all went quiet for a few weeks until the next email was sent mid-April. But this time it had been sent to HMRC."

Both Agnes and Delores raised eyebrows. Ellen nodded. "Quite. You both own your own businesses. You know how tough it is dealing with HMRC. The slightest whiff of financial irregularity and they're straight on you."

"What did the email say this time?" asked Delores.

"It was from someone claiming to be a whistle-blower who told them we had two sets of books, and we were only declaring part of our financial dealings."

"That's a serious allegation," said Delores.

"Beyond serious," said Ellen, "and completely untrue. But as you can imagine, it caused havoc. HMRC sent in not one but two sets of external auditors. They interviewed everyone, went through the ledgers (historic and current), every single transaction in detail. Absolute forensic financial audits. The two different auditors compared what they had been told to see if they could catch us out. They checked with our wholesale and retail customers and all our suppliers. It was just awful. It was horrible. But there was nothing to find. No matter how hard they looked, and trust me, they looked hard, there was nothing hidden. Nothing missing. Everything was and still is above board. But once that trust is broken, or damaged in our case, it doesn't really come back. It's like we're still under suspicion and we've just got to live with it."

"Surely Charles couldn't ignore this one, it's far too serious," said Agnes.

"He continues to be unshakeable in his belief that no one would maliciously hurt the business. His grandfather's influence and faith in people still runs strong in Charles and shapes how he thinks and behaves to this day. He just won't hear a bad word against anyone."

"But the flip side of that makes it seem like he's willing to risk the family business just because of an honourable, if slightly unrealistic, view of the world," said Agnes.

Ellen shrugged her shoulders. "I agree but can you see now what I've been dealing with? I can't get anywhere with him but I'm just not going to ignore this or bury my head in the sand anymore."

"What was Charlie's reaction this time?" asked Delores.

"His words were not to push him because we didn't know what else he was capable of."

"Not exactly the words of an innocent person, are they?" said Agnes. "Ellen, do you really think Charlie was responsible for the emails?"

"He had access to all of the company information and our systems, so yes, it's possible, but he's my son. Our son. As much as I don't want it to be him, there's a niggling voice that keeps telling me it's him. He's getting more and more frustrated that Charles isn't going anywhere and that the clock's ticking. But sometimes the best I can tell myself as his mother, is that he's all mouth and no trousers. It doesn't make me feel good thinking about him in this way or make me feel confident for the long-term future of the company once he does inherit. But right now, right here as his mother, I'd rather think of him as a somewhat unpleasant, mouthy, entitled man child, as opposed to someone deliberately trying to destroy not just his family, but the business and the livelihoods of everyone who works there, just because he's having a temper tantrum that he's not getting his own way. But I've always got this merry-go-round in my head... it's him... it's not him... it's him... it's not him... The more I try to ignore the noise, the louder and more persistent it gets."

"You said things had been happening all year," said Agnes. "Did the emails continue?"

"Actually, thinking of emails," said Delores, "I clearly need to change my password, Agnes, if you were able to access my laptop."

"Absolutely," said Agnes rolling her eyes, "if you think that will help… but yes, we do need to catch up on that later." Delores frowned but Agnes just mouthed 'later' to her. "Apologies, Ellen, carry on."

"No, they stopped," said Ellen. "I was telling Delores before you arrived that it's been a year of horrible events, but there were no more emails after the HMRC one thankfully, so I thought that was that and tried to move on from a horrible few months, but that changed in summer."

"What happened then?" asked Agnes.

"We've got three delivery trucks. Two of them were in the garage for servicing so we were down to just one. We were totally reliant on it, but we came into work one day to find the tyres had been slashed. Every single tyre on it."

"But surely you have CCTV in your yard?" interrupted Agnes.

Ellen shook her head. "No, afraid not. No CCTV anywhere. It's been suggested on many an occasion, but each time Charles says no. Back to his belief in the people who work here and a refusal to think they do anything bad."

Agnes sighed. "I get the sentiment, Ellen, I really do. But it's a bad business decision not to have it for this very reason."

"I know, but what can I do? Charles just won't budge."

"Was it just the truck targeted?" asked Delores.

Ellen shook her head. "No. I wish it was – I mean that's bad enough, but we also had all the keys to the forklifts go missing on a big despatch day when we had major orders to get out."

"Could that just have been bad luck in your transport office with the keys going missing? A one-off?"

"I told myself at the time, maybe it was that. But then we had flavour labels getting mixed up on the seasonings, so the crisps were made with the wrong flavourings. Luckily, the QC team found it before the orders were despatched, but we had to dispose of everything, do a complete shutdown, major clean and a QC of every single ingredient in the manufacturing line."

Agnes shuddered. "Just think, there you are, Delores, with your favourite pack of Prawn Cocktail crisps anticipating the joy they'll bring you, but you end up with a mouthful of crunchy Cajun Squirrel instead."

Delores managed to turn both pale and green at the same time whilst eyeing with considerable suspicion the pack of Prawn Cocktail crisps she'd taken out of the box that Ellen brought. Maybe she should first offer one to Agnes just to check there weren't any rampant squirrels inside.

"Don't mock it," said Ellen, "Cajun Squirrel really was a flavour (though not one of ours in our defence). Short lived to be fair. I don't think too many people upon seeing a squirrel would immediately wonder what seasoning it would be best paired with."

"Clearly someone did and clearly that person should not be involved in future taste tests," said Delores, still shuddering with horror.

"There wasn't actual squirrel in the ingredients," said Ellen. "No squirrels were harmed in the making of those savoury snacks." Delores, still not convinced, definitely decided to nominate Agnes as her personal taste tester for all crunchy-based snack foods henceforth.

Ellen continued. "We then found on one shift that glue had been put into the potato slicer. It had completely seized up. So that was another two days' lost production whilst we got in new parts and fixed the machine. Then, we had orders to suppliers being cancelled and some even had payments blocked as well… We've worked so hard to rebuild the trust after those fake financial emails that after this we were almost back at square one again. We had to drop everything and reassure our suppliers that all was well and then process ultra-fast payments to them which the bank did not appreciate."

"From what you've said so far," said Agnes, "the immediate conclusion is that it's definitely an inside job. There simply can't be an external force in play."

"I agree," said Delores, "but by not taking things seriously at the start of the year, you've ended up in a much worse situation."

"But that's not the end of it though, it gets worse," said Ellen.

"How can it get worse?" asked Delores.

"Secret Santa happened," said Ellen.

"Secret Santa?" asked Agnes. "I remember those from my old office job in London. I got a useless calendar once."

"Why was it useless?" asked Delores.

"It was four years out of date," said Agnes, "but at least it wasn't a hamster which someone deemed a suitable gift for one of the receptionists. I don't know who screamed louder… the hamster or her. The hamster made a run for it and was never seen again, closely followed by the receptionist. After that, the company decided to pause Secret Santa indefinitely due to 'unforeseen trauma.'"

"Okay, yep I agree, an out-of-date calendar is pretty useless as gifts go, but far better than a live rodent. What happened at your Secret Santa, Ellen?" said Delores.

"We've done Secret Santa for about ten years now; didn't do it last year but wanted a bit of normality this year. But when the second lockdown was announced in October to start in November, we reconsidered and pretty much were going to cancel, but then decided if we were careful and got anyone who wanted to do it to leave their gifts one at a time and then on the day itself open our 'gifts' in the car park, it meant we were all in the open air and could stay a good two metres away from each other. Just like the first lockdown we remained open so thought it would be good for staff morale."

"I assume it wasn't?" asked Delores.

"No," said Ellen, "not at all. It's open to all in the company, but not everyone wants to join in. That's fine, there's no pressure. Charles's PA arranges it every year; takes care of everything so it runs smoothly. There was a discussion of postponing the gift exchange until after the lockdown had ended, but as we remained open and had staff in working, we went ahead. There were only about eighteen or so people in it, and most got the usual kind of gift, but six didn't. Six people received gifts that can only be described as unpleasant... some of the side effects were just nasty, too nasty to be considered 'joke gifts.'"

"In what way?" asked Delores.

"Well at face value it was strange really, as the six are all in different departments and at different levels within the company. In fact, apart from working at the same factory, there's no link between any of them, only the fact they all took part in Secret Santa. There's Daniel Smythe to start with; works in the Transport Office. He got a big box of chocolates, which we all thought was a really nice gift as he's a renowned chocolate lover. He opened them straight away and dug straight in, but shortly after he'd eaten his way through about half the box he started to suffer from... how to say this politely... stomach cramps, and, well, a rather gurgling bubbly sensation in the lower stomach area."

"Are we talking a Code Brown?" asked Delores.

Ellen nodded. "Yes, a rather sudden full-on brutal liquid Code Brown." Delores made a mental note to herself not to open the new bar of chocolate that she had hidden away in the back of the workshop... or preferably get Agnes to try it first.

Ellen continued. "Then there was Jason Sadler, the factory manager. He was given what we thought was a very nice pen. And what does everyone do when they get a pen? You try it, don't you? Well, the second he started to write, the pen exploded, and his hand was covered in blue ink."

"Could the pen have just been faulty?" asked Agnes.

"We've all inadvertently ended up with ink-stained hands from dodgy pens."

"No," said Ellen, "on closer inspection, we saw that the pen had holes in it for the ink to deliberately come out of… his hands are still blue."

"I know that feeling," said Delores. "Last month I dyed my hands Sky Blue. It was a right pain to try and wash it off, but on the bright side the ribbons I was dying came out beautifully. Even if I did not." Delores looked down at her hands and like Lady Macbeth was sure she could still see a tinge of blue.

"Then there was Alice Alderman," continued Ellen. "She got a lovely toiletries set. She's always buying the latest beauty products and part of her gift was some talcum powder. Well she tried it straight away, but seconds after liberally coating her arms she started to itch. And then her skin turned bright red. Then it got angry hot and blotchy."

"Itching powder?" suggested Agnes.

"Yes," said Ellen, "itching powder. Then there was Lee Turner, one of our lorry drivers. A bag full of sweets was his gift, and it's also known he has a sweet tooth. He opened them straight away, popped two in his mouth and seconds later blood started to gush."

Agnes and Delores looked horrified. In unison they both said, "Blood!!!"

"Well, we all thought it was blood, but the sweets had some sort of red liquid in them. So when the sugar coating cracked open, the liquid made his mouth water to the point where it just looked like pools of blood were pouring from his mouth. It was horrible."

"I can imagine," said Delores, making another mental

note to either throw away or give to Agnes the sweets she usually offered her clients. "So that's four people who were targeted; who else?"

"Lizzie and Charles also had rather nasty surprises, although Lizzie's was the worst. Charles's gift is more of a mystery than anything else."

"Why's that?" asked Agnes.

"Well, Lizzie's gift was a set of three lipsticks, all shades of red; her go-to colour. She tried the first one but wiped it off quite quickly as it made her lips sting. So, she tried another, but the same thing happened. Then she tried the third, but straight away we could all see her lips turn bright red and start to burn. Honestly, I could see them blister in front of me. It was nasty."

"Was there something in the lipsticks that caused the burn?" asked Delores. "Is Lizzie allergic to anything?"

"She's allergic to chilli peppers and when we had a closer look at them, we saw dried crushed chilli flakes mixed into the lipsticks. God knows which type of chilli it was, but the burn was instantaneous," said Ellen.

"So what about Charles?" asked Agnes.

"His gift was more odd than anything else. It read like a joke to begin with, but as Charles opened his last and after the previous unpleasant incidents, it then just seemed like an unfunny threat against him."

"What did he get?" asked Agnes.

"It was a jigsaw puzzle, not many pieces. A white background with a phrase printed on it. The letters were printed backwards, but when the puzzle was complete and the letters written the right way round, it said 'I know what you did. You will pay'. It makes no sense.

Neither Charles nor I have any idea what it's referring to."

"Do you believe him?" asked Agnes. "Even after the year that you've had?"

"Yes, genuinely I do. There's never been any secrets between us, we've been lucky. Neither of us has a clue what he's supposed to have done."

"So that's six people targeted," said Agnes. "No one else?"

Ellen shook her head. "Just the six."

"Sounds more like Satan Santa than Secret Santa," said Agnes, "although Secret Santa Slays Six works just as well."

"I really, really need your help to find out who's done all this," said Ellen, adding, "and why."

"Even if it's Charlie?" asked Delores.

"Even if it's Charlie," said Ellen. "Whoever the person is, this has to stop now before someone really gets hurt. The Secret Santa presents caused discomfort, but it could've been much worse, and I don't want it getting any worse. It's got to stop now."

Agnes and Delores agreed.

"What we need to do next, Ellen, is write all of this up, whiteboard the key points and people and then decide how we go about the investigation. Are you okay to leave it with us for a day or two? Delores will be in touch if we need any more information, but I think we have enough to start," said Agnes.

Ellen agreed, and tearfully thanking Agnes and Delores, she left them to it. As she was about to leave, she paused at the door, turning round to face them. She said, "You've got quite a task ahead of you. I'm so sorry to put this on you."

"Don't worry," said Delores, "it's what we do."

"Indeed we do," said Agnes. "We're going to find Santa."

After Delores had shown Ellen out and locked the door behind her, she turned back to Agnes.

"What do you think we should do first?"

Agnes twiddled her pen, mentally working out a plan in her head before replying.

"It's late but I'll go over to the office and replay this conversation from the recording. I'll whiteboard the key events, timelines and people and we'll go from there. But the single most urgent need is to get in there and interview everyone, take some photos and maybe get some fingerprints."

"Excellent," said Delores, "a show-and-tell workplace event. Gotta love one of those!"

"And of course with mince pies and hot chocolates," said Agnes. "Disposable plates and cups of course, naturally for 'recycling afterwards', but we'll insist on taking everything away with us when we clear up and then see what we can lift from them."

"Naturally," said Delores. "Maybe we could get the ladies in to go on a tour of the business as well. The intelligence they can gather with no one noticing could be invaluable."

"Sounds like a plan," said Agnes, now with her coat on and ready to leave. "Okay, so shall we debrief tomorrow lunchtime for first pass planning? I've got some baking to do in the morning but then Zelda's coming in for the afternoon so that'll free me up."

"Sounds good to me," said Delores. "That'll give me a chance in the morning to get my Zoom session in with Monsieur Delvene."

"What's he showing you this time?" asked Agnes.

"French techniques of cloche hat making from the 1910s, specifically the life and legacy of Catherine Reboux, 'La Grande Dame' as Monsieur calls her. She was a legend, a trendsetter who left a lasting legacy which I think is what he's trying to do to me, although God knows why. I'm convinced there are times that he thinks I don't have any talent at all based on some of his facial expressions."

"Well, have fun with that," said Agnes, "I wonder if she used staples."

Delores grimaced. "One day, you *will* learn to use a sewing machine and break free from the staple gun."

"And the next day, dear Delores, you *will* learn how to make meringues and break free from buying them from a supermarket," replied Agnes.

Delores laughed. "Anyway, changing the subject, talk to me about my laptop."

"Ahhhhh yes, your laptop," said Agnes. "I got an alert the other week that 'someone' had been trying to access the millinery, bakery and agency computers, so I double-checked your laptop just to make sure all was okay."

"Was it?" asked Delores.

"Oh yes, the encryption I've used for everything is Security Services grade. But seriously, if you do change your password, don't choose the name of one of your pets again."

"Was it that obvious?" asked Delores.

"Using the name of your late cat who hated you? Didn't take long to work out," said Agnes.

"You know I lost count of the number of times that cat tried to kill me," said Delores. "He's still trying."

"What now? Even from 'the other side'?" said Agnes.

"Yep," said Delores, "I swear he's come back as an undead zombie ghost cat to have another go at me. Tell me, how come the other day when I was coming down the stairs, I found, five steps from the bottom, his favourite squeaky ball? Seriously, he's still trying to make me fall down the stairs and break my neck. Even in death, that damn cat still hates me."

"Well, luckily for me," said Agnes, "I avoid all animals, domestic and wild, so only you seem to have a deceased cat assassin. Although there was that one time I got chased round the village green by that goose. No idea what had possessed it, but it was clearly having some sort of manic rage episode and I got caught up in the crossfire. Quacking awful, it was. Quacking."

"Well, quite," said Delores, "but back to the hacker. Did you find out who they were and what they wanted?"

"In reverse order. The 'why'… I don't know. They had a good root round but couldn't get into any of our secure files for any of the businesses. All the data is securely encrypted, so nothing was accessed. As for the 'who'? They did a good job of masking their location, but my software is better. They were bouncing their location all around the globe, but I tracked all the pings, and they led back to one location, the place of which is rather intriguing. So I've been running a few more checks in the background, but I might need to go on a bit of a road trip to work out the 'who' at the 'where'. They did leave an interesting calling card though embedded on the agency server."

"What did it say?" asked Delores.

"Armadillo," said Agnes.

Four

Friday, 3rd December 2021

The next morning dawned bright and early for Delores. She had a couple of jobs to do in the workshop before her 10a.m. call with Monsieur Delvene. She knew he despised lateness, so she always dialled in at 9:56a.m.

Delores often wondered why she was friends with Monsieur Delvene and why she had these coaching sessions with him. It was often a love-hate relationship, he was without doubt an expert in his field, and if he didn't know something, it wasn't worth knowing, so his mentoring was invaluable. But he was also the one person who was brutally honest with Delores if he didn't like something she'd made, or if he disagreed with her creative thought process. On many an occasion, Delores had proudly shown him her latest piece, only to be met with varying degrees of '*Non!*'. It ranged from mild '*Non!*' meaning, I don't like it, to a firmer '*Non!*', plus flared nostril, indicating positive hatred. To a tonally specific '*Non!*' with a flared nostril *and* a raised eyebrow, which indicated total and utter outrage at the piece and that

Delores should reconsider her life choices and take up an entirely different career.

Deep down, Delores knew that he did this with the best of intentions, and it made her a better milliner. It made her finished headpieces even better, but it was hard to hear sometimes. Delores recalled one occasion, after working through the night, showing Monsieur the finished article, only to receive not just one tonally specific '*Non!*' but three *and* with a flared nostril *and* a raised eyebrow but also followed by his hand banging on the table three times, finishing with a finger waggle and a final '*Non!*' to get his point across. Delores, bereft of sleep and coffee, proceeded to tell Monsieur Delvene exactly what she thought of him and which of his orifices her steamer would be inserted the next time she saw him. Followed by a detailed tirade of how she would make use of her hot glue gun, and how his eyebrows, nostrils and fingers would be removed whilst using it. Luckily for Delores, the benefit of being bereft of sleep and coffee also meant she didn't realise she was on mute, and all Monsieur saw was a passionate, if silent, mouthing of a response, with many hand gestures which he interpreted as Delores explaining to him what changes she would make.

Monsieur Delvene knew that Delores was talented and knew she needed to be challenged sometimes to bring out her fighting spirit and top game. So he also knew exactly what he was doing when he said '*Non!*' and exactly what he was doing when his response was '*C'est parfait!*'.

Delores dialled in first, bang on 9:56a.m. and within thirty seconds, Monsieur appeared on screen. He was, as ever, impeccably dressed, perfectly coordinated, wellgroomed in a bespoke, tailor-made three-piece suit with a perfectly pressed shirt and natty bow tie. Not a hair out of place. Delores was grateful that Monsieur could only see her top half on screen, and he couldn't see the two pairs of thermal leggings, mismatched socks, one white trainer and one slightly dyed trainer in various shades of blue, green and orange which Delores had worn last week to dye feathers. Monsieur still gave the top half of Delores a look up and down, and she began to panic when he subconsciously patted his perfectly groomed hair. Her face beginning to go pink, then red, then puce could not disguise her panic at what he might have been looking at. Slowly, she raised her left hand to her head and patted gently. Out fell four crystals, eighteen sequins, a pencil and two shells (beach not grenade).

"Good morning, *monsieur*," Delores spluttered.

"Good morning, *madame*," he replied, nostrils flared at half-mast. *Not the best of starts*, thought Delores.

After the polite pleasantries had concluded, Monsieur asked Delores for an update on the pieces she was working on for a Norwich theatre company. Their pantomime this year was *Cinderella and the Socially Distanced Pumpkin* for which Delores was making eight headpieces, each with a shoe on top to represent Cinderella's glass slipper. The first show was this upcoming Saturday, and the pieces were being collected tomorrow, so quite frankly, it was too late to change anything, even if Monsieur didn't like them.

One by one, Delores showed him the pieces, the first, a black sequin-covered-four-inch-open-toed sandal with a bow front and back and a black felt ankle strap. Somewhat nervously Delores asked, "What are your thoughts, *monsieur*?"

Monsieur didn't reply. There was just silence; no movement from him whatsoever. Delores considered if this was a thoughtful silence as he composed his thoughts, or a deadly silence as he planned a list of all the things he hated. Or had the screen just frozen? She jumped when clearly it wasn't the screen that had frozen. Monsieur came to life and suddenly said, "Tell me your processes and techniques."

"Oh, um, right, okay," said Delores, trying to regain the ability to put thoughts in brain together with words in mouth. "Okay, well I, designed the shoe and constructed the shape in cardboard. I then covered the base in black felt and stitched them together." Delores paused to look at the expression on Monsieur's face and wished she hadn't as it was totally blank. Her internal panic dial was moving from Normal to Marginally Alarmed, but she continued, "I then created the front and heel section from felt and stitched them to the base. Once this was done, I covered the shoe with a black sequin material and added the bow and feathers." As Delores continued to explain the techniques, Monsieur's expression changed from nothing, to frowning deep thought, to pursed lips, to stone cold nothing. The internal panic dial had now moved from Marginally Alarmed to Just a Bit Terrified, but she persisted. "My next step was to block a base for the shoe to sit on using buckram. I then stitched wire to the inside edge and covered the base in pink velour." Monsieur blinked on the word 'pink'; Delores's mind was racing… was this a normal blink, a confused blink, an angry blink, or a what-the-hell-do-you-think-you're-doing blink? Her internal panic dial had now moved from Just a Bit Terrified to Actually Quite Scared Now, but she took a breath and continued. "I stitched a Petersham band on the inside and attached the shoe to the base. Once this was securely attached, I added a lining to the inside of the hat base and a headband so it's wearable. *Et voilà*, one headpiece." As the words '*et voilà*' left her mouth, Delores began to regret using them to an actual French man. Internal panic dial now set at the maximum level of I'm Going to Spontaneously Combust.

Delores also seriously regretted her choice of wearing man-made fibres on this call and was so flustered she didn't notice that Monsieur had started talking or what he had said, or when he then stopped talking. She resorted to nodding her head before uttering the classic line…

"Sorry, you broke up a bit on that last bit. Would you mind repeating?"

Monsieur did not look happy, but he gave a nod and condensed his feedback into…

"*Oui, madame.* Your pieces are acceptable, most appropriate for the stage." Delores nearly fell off her chair. This was high praise from Monsieur.

Monsieur continued, "You need to push yourself, Delores. You are most capable, but your self-doubt takes over and holds you back. You must be bold! Let yourself go in the creative process! Be more Reboux!"

With each phrase, Monsieur was getting increasingly passionate and his accent increasingly more French. "La Grande Madame pushed the boundaries with her bold fashion pieces. Like her, you can design and make a perfectly coordinated matching headpiece to any outfit, couture or high street, but Le Grand Madame went further. There may have been times she doubted what she was doing. After all, she opened her first shop in 1865, an achievement for a woman back then. And then she started to design and produce high-fashion pieces, statement pieces challenging the views of women's millinery. Like you, she started out as an apprentice, learning from experts. You have that same shared start, the same expert training. You just need to believe in yourself, *madame*. It just takes one piece worn at the right event to change your life. So keep with the passion, keep pushing the boundaries. *Believe in yourself!*"

It was quite the speech and Delores felt worn out with it all, so she was relieved that the rest of the hour's session passed quickly and as ever a stickler for being on time, Monsieur also believed in punctuality in ending a call. At 10.59a.m., farewells were made, a date in the diary for their next catch-up agreed and *bang*, ever the whirlwind he was gone. Restoring her sanity with a cup of tea and a slice of Agnes's Battenburg cake she regained her composure until it was time to head off to the detective agency.

The agency was based in an office above a storage garage Agnes used to store 'stuff'. Sometimes it was better not to ask what she stored there and even if you did ask, Agnes would just say 'stuff'. But it didn't take Delores long to get there from her workshop. It was accessed by a separate front door (fingerprint and iris scanner) but there was also a hidden side-entrance door (face recognition, fingerprint, iris scanner, pin code and invisible door laser alarms) for those times Delores and Agnes, or their clients, needed a discreet way in or out to avoid any prying eyes at the main entrance.

Accessing the office by the side door, Delores found Agnes bringing out a plateful of salted caramel cookies and the kettle just coming to the boil.

"Good morning?" asked Agnes.

"Good morning and yes, a good morning, well at least it was a morning where I didn't spontaneously combust," replied Delores.

"Ahhhh, so your session with Monsieur Delvene went well then."

"As well as these things do," said Delores, looking round at the whiteboards Agnes had pulled out. "Do you want to talk me through it?"

Agnes began...

"One of the challenges we have here, is that some of these events happened months ago. Witnesses and evidence will be difficult to get hold of, Ellen said they'd reported some details to Yarmouth Police Station so it might be useful to see if we can find a paper trail there. There's only the briefest of records uploaded to the police database, covering the date and time they went out and why they were called out, but it also states that no further action would be taken. I'm hoping more paperwork will be in a filing box somewhere, but I also very much doubt it. The emails sent from Crispin Crisps' server will still be hidden on them somewhere – a 'delete' isn't ever a real delete unless you do a real deep dive, but it would be best to log onto one of their computers on their server." Agnes paused for a sip of tea and a bite of her salted caramel cookie... *needs more salt...* she noted to herself.

She continued out loud, "Secret Santa is the most recent incident so this should be the easiest event to start with and if we can find Santa, we can then work backwards to see if we can link him or her to the events earlier in the year."

"I agree," said Delores. "Whoever this was, and it *will* be an inside job, has got a massive problem with the company to cause nearly a year's worth of problems so he, or she, can definitely hold a grudge."

"I've whiteboarded the relevant facts as we know them," said Agnes, walking over to the first of the electronic whiteboards and flipping it round. "This is the management board at Crispin Crisps: Charles III, owner and Managing Director, with Anne Mayhew as his PA. Then, wife Ellen (Finance Director), son Charlie (General Director and heir), daughter Lizzie (Supply Chain Director), younger brother CC (Marketing Director), Malcolm Carson (New Product Director), Jayne Johns (Legal Director) and Richard Coates (HR Director) bringing up the rear."

"That's a beautiful-looking whiteboard diagram," said Delores.

"You ain't seen nothing yet," replied Agnes. "Now we come onto whiteboard number two and the timeline of events."

Agnes flipped the second whiteboard around which detailed:

Tuesday 19th January – Email from bank re loan implications.
Friday 12th February – Email from journalist.
Friday 9th April – HMRC: first contact.

Tuesday 13th to Tuesday 20th April – Auditors and HMRC investigation.
Saturday 19th to Sunday 20th June – Tyres slashed.
Tuesday 6th July – Fork lift keys go missing.
Thursday 12th August – Flavour mix-up.
Thursday 26th August – Slicer glued.
Thursday 9th September – Supplier orders cancelled, and payments blocked.
Monday 1st November – Secret Santa invites.
Thursday 25th November – Secret Santa presents handed in.
Friday 26th November – Secret Santa event takes place.
Wednesday 1st December – Ellen's visit to Delores.

Delores took a moment to study the dates and the notes.

"So there have been eight months where 'events' have happened. Looking at them… mainly weekdays, no Wednesdays though (could be important), but no obvious pattern. Nothing in March, May or October so we'll need to see all the holiday and sickness records to work out if the same person was maybe off during these months, but truthfully, I think that's unlikely."

"Agreed," said Agnes. "It's as if whoever did this started small with the email campaign then waited for the fallout. When none was forthcoming, he or she moved onto HMRC. Now that certainly did cause a significant interruption with the auditors coming in but apart from damage to brand reputation there was nothing to find. So then we've got four months where individually the events aren't that bad, but they're coming thick and quick causing major disruption to the entire operation."

"Then nothing in October," said Delores, "waiting again for any fallout over the last four months' campaign and once again thwarted."

"And then we come onto the latest incident. Possibly now completely wound up that there's been no change to the business and Crispin Crisps remains untouchable, the perpetrator ups their game and gets personal. The invites for Secret Santa went out on the 1st of November (Ellen wasn't wrong, they did go early this year), with an instruction that all gifts were to be placed in a meeting room next to the canteen by close of business on the 25th of November. The gifts were then moved into the canteen on the 26th under the tree ready for the Secret Santa reveal later that afternoon in the car park. Which brings me onto whiteboard three," said Agnes, twirling round to the next whiteboard and flipping it round.

"Loving your work," said Delores, "but are those toilet door images?"

"Certainly are," said Agnes, far prouder than she probably ought to be. "I thought they added a nice touch of 'order' to the display."

"You've got back door access to every government database going, plus every single social media account in existence to find actual photos!"

"Trust me, 'back door' access would be the easy route. Sometimes it's more a case of 'open the front door, down the garden path, get in the car, arrive at the airport, board an aeroplane to somewhere hot... or cold... trade in copious amounts of camels, or reindeer or vodka, then get back on an aeroplane, back in the car, back up the front path and re-enter the front door'. Back door access is easier but sometimes not always the right way to get what you need."

"Well that certainly explains why you know more than is normal about camel racing." Agnes nodded in agreement.

"You've not lived until you've stood in front of a camel coming at you at forty miles per hour. And then if you don't get out of the way pretty sharpish you won't live for much longer. What a statement to end up on your death certificate... 'Death by camel'. Anyway, most of the time you don't need access to secure databases, it's frightening how many people on social media don't have any privacy controls set up. Their profiles are open for anyone to view and they're posting every moment from their lives. Where they are, what they're doing, what they're eating, how long they'll be on holiday, their front door, their back door, how they've redecorated, who they live with and where they work. It's alarming how people don't seem to realise what they're sharing, but incredibly helpful when data mining."

"Well quite," said Delores, but it was no good – Agnes was on a rant and there was no stopping her.

"...And then... then we go onto the photos posted... heavily filtered, flattering soft lighting applied and you name it they've photographed and posted it, but search through enough online pictures and on professional work sites and more often than not a 'real' picture of what they look like can be found."

"Have you finished now?" asked Delores – Agnes

nodded and paused for a breath. Delores continued, "*Death by Camel* would definitely make for an interesting talking point at the funeral. But seriously, do you have the actual photos?"

Agnes laughed and said, "For you..." and pressed a button on a remote control. The whiteboards updated and as if by magic the photos appeared.

"I'm not sure whether to be impressed by that or disturbed," said Delores.

"Be both," said Agnes, "then you've covered all bases."

"So how are we going to play this?" asked Delores. "We're Friday now and Ellen mentioned they're having a Christmas bazaar in the car park on Monday. It was looking doubtful at one stage but with lockdown being lifted there's a few local businesses going in the hope they get a Christmas boost to their sales after struggling for almost two years now. I take it we'll be there as well?"

"Definitely," said Agnes. "It's the ideal time to get the ladies in and I've got Marjory Bartlett coming in shortly to go through a plan of action for the day. So if you do your usual display stand, I'll do the refreshments and we'll get the ladies to go round with a nibbles trolley to get the insider intelligence. Then we can meet up afterwards for a debrief and update of the boards."

"Sounds good and I can test drive my new free-standing banner and mannequin heads at the event as well. Hope it doesn't rain though. You know I'd really like to try and get this one wrapped up as soon as possible for Ellen. She's had a horrible year and we're fairly quiet at the moment so we (and Ellen) may be in luck."

"A) I agree," said Agnes, "and b) 'wrapped up'... as in Secret Santa wrapped up?"

Delores snorted a laugh. "Unintentional but absolutely, yes. We've only got the five missing cat cases at the moment, so a quick win on this one would be good."

"Four," said Agnes. "Mr Tibbles has been found."

"Really? Where?" asked Delores.

"Manchester," said Agnes. Delores looked confused.

"Manchester? How in the cat's fluff did he get there?"

"The neighbour was having some work done and one of the contractors was from Manchester. I gave them a quick call and it turned out that Mr Tibbles had decided to stow away in the contractor's van when he left. The contractor apparently found him in the van a few days after returning home, miraculously fully fed and watered and quite content with life but he'll be reunited with Mrs Miggins soon."

"Just to clarify, you mean the cat and not the contractor," said Delores.

"That would be Mr Tibbles."

"Well I'm pleased to hear it. So that leaves us with four cases and Ellen. Although I do have leads on Timmy and Pickles and potentially Snowball's a possibility too."

"Sounds promising, although if the owners had leads on the cats to start with, they may not have gone missing in the first place, but aside from that what have you found?" asked Agnes.

"Timmy and Pickles have been sighted back in Oulton Broad, where the family used to live, and Snowball appears to have taken up residence in the Foodco Extra store on the other side of Yarmouth; by all accounts, he's living the dream with a stream of customers and staff feeding him *and* he's got a warm place to sleep on the lottery counter. It's just Nigel who is proving to be an enigma."

"That's 'Nigels' for you," said Agnes. "Law unto themselves, but getting back to Ellen, I think we need to attend the bazaar using our day-to-day business endeavours and see what we can find. As long as I can access one of their computers this weekend, I can quickly do some digging on the emails and then between us all we can see what we can find out about Secret Santa. We also need to take a look at the factory and yard but I'm hoping Ellen can get us in on Sunday when no one's around so we can have a good look without anyone noticing."

"Okay, sounds good to me."

"In the meantime, I need to take a road trip tomorrow. I need to scratch an armadillo hunch."

"Well that sounds like you're in need of a vet instead of a road trip," said Delores. "I know Ellen, Charles and Crispin have gone to an exhibition in Norwich today so you might not hear back that quickly for Sunday access."

"Not to worry, I'll text her tomorrow if I don't hear back sooner."

The security camera alert gave a sudden tingle to indicate someone was approaching the front door. Agnes and Delores both looked up at the monitor to see Marjory approaching with Edith and Esme in tow. The doorbell buzzed and Delores went down to let them in. Agnes popped the kettle on and emptied a selection of cookies, pastries and more packs of crisps from the box that Ellen gave to Delores onto a large plate. After all, a meeting without tea and nibbles was a crime in itself.

It only took a few minutes for the visitors to settle in and once supplied with hot steaming tea and the small mountain of nibbles, Agnes and Delores took them through the latest case.

"From what you've said," began Marjory, "it does seem like an inside job but are you totally ruling out outside interference?"

"We're ninety percent certain it's an inside job," said Delores. "Whoever did this needed to know about the company's financial position, the day-to-day workings of the factory and the Secret Santa plans. So even someone outside the company would still need an insider to get them the information."

"Okay, so our focus on Monday is watching the staff up close and getting the insider view on what's really going on there," said Marjory, "so it's a Tea and Biscuits con on the trolley to get fingerprints." Marjory paused and looked at Edith and Esme. "And what do we do, ladies, if someone says they don't want a drink or nibble?"

"Drop an empty cup because we are old and fumble a lot…" said Edith.

"…And wait for their reflexes to kick in and catch it," finished Esme.

"Absolutely," said Marjory. "Their reflexes will subconsciously kick in, so they'll catch it and hand it back without realising. That's the beauty of the Tea and Biscuits… we'll get them either way." Marjory looked back at Delores.

"Do you need any help with the Stitch and Run?"

"Potentially a few models would be good, I'll also pick out some pieces for you to wear (from the men's and ladies' range) and then when you're at my stall if you can encourage any passing staff to try them on then bag and tag any stray hairs that would be very helpful indeed."

"Do you need any photos?" asked Edith. "We can also run a Kodak Moment to get them."

"An oldie but a goodie," said Esme. "One of us will whip out a smartphone and pretend we can't take photos or selfies, so a well-meaning poor sap will step in to 'help'. By the time they've shown us, we've completely captured the entire area."

"And with three or four old ladies all running a Kodak Moment in different areas we'll get everything," said Edith.

"As many photos as possible please," said Delores. "You'll be able to get people off guard, so we might get something very useful."

"It sounds like we have a plan," said Agnes. "Marjory, if you can round up the troops and meet us at the factory for 12p.m. on Monday, Delores and I will be ready with the stands, trolleys and various accoutrements we need for a successful mission."

And with that the plan was hatched.

Five

Saturday, 4th December 2021

Agnes spent a couple of hours in the bakery early on Saturday morning, making sure all the bakes and cakes were in full supply for the day ahead. She knew she was lucky to have enough staff who could run the place when the detective agency needed her time. Agnes planned out with the bakery manager what needed to be done for the rest of Saturday as well as an ingredient walk-through for Monday.

It might not have been the biggest bakery but even though tourist season had ended, the Christmas bakes were in full flow and on more than one occasion, the staff were very impressed, along with just a bit mystified when customers came in and bought thirty-six mince pies, five yule logs and twenty-four Santa cupcakes on a single order regular basis. They decided that even with this year's Christmas restrictions, everyone in their three households meeting up over the five-day Christmas break would be eating two years' worth of Christmas fayre.

Around 10a.m., Agnes set off on her Armadillo

mission. Her software had all pointed to the external access attempts coming from the same location, so she knew the 'where' if not the exact 'where' at the where. As to the 'who' and 'why'... the 'who' could be anyone and based on the 'where' her mind raced with possibilities. She knew the 'why' would be inextricably linked to the 'who' and again based on where the 'where' was, her mind was in overdrive. Agnes also realised that if anyone ever tried to put her thoughts on paper for someone to read, she'd likely be sent to an institution for the permanently befuddled of mind, but she rested easy knowing that at least it made sense to her.

Agnes decided to take the coastal roads to get to her intended destination to make it a nice trip out. The North Sea might not be sparkling turquoise blue, but it was still impressive and even though she saw the sea every day, it still made her happy to see the sea on her journey. It would take a good two hours to get to the 'where' and that was without traffic and any stops, but Agnes was in no hurry. The place where she was going was in theory closed for the winter, but she still had a plan in mind.

The winter Norfolk roads were quiet, so Agnes was able to take in the views (whilst, for the record, remaining in full control of her car), passing through small villages with their flint-covered cottages a sight synonymous with the Norfolk countryside. Flint had been a cornerstone (pun intended) here for tens of thousands of years; you'd find it in ancient tools found by archaeologists, castle ruins, city walls, crumbling priories and walls of old and new cottages. To Agnes, the flint meant Norfolk and Norfolk meant home. Agnes never lost her sense of awe at the views around her and knew she'd never swap her new life for her old one in London.

Pausing briefly at Happisburgh to look at the red and white lighthouse, she marvelled in the fact that despite being built in 1790 it was still working and still shining its light out across the sea. Agnes wondered how many people through the centuries had seen the lighthouse, either by land or sea and how many lives it had saved. It was a sobering thought as she carried on her journey.

Agnes decided to take a break at Cromer. There was a car park on Runton Road which was always a good place to stop off, and out of season would have plenty of available parking. There was also a good cut-through down to the esplanade and pier, although Agnes would avoid at all costs buying anything crab related. She held a firm belief that it was not normal to eat an animal that was essentially a massive spider in a hard shell. That was a no thank you, move straight to dessert moment. The car park also had a clear view over to the holiday park where the caravans over the years had got ever closer to the edge of the sandy cliffs, the sight of which both impressed and alarmed Agnes.

After a power walk to and back from the pier in the cloudy 7-degree chilly wind Agnes was happy to get back in the car and carry on with her mission. Still determined to follow the coast road, Agnes carried on and travelled through Sheringham on her way to Cley Windmill, in Cley next the Sea. As well as flint, the windmill was another Norfolk fixture; a common sight to lots of people travelling on the broads and beyond. Agnes tried to think of the number of windmills still in Norfolk. She'd read somewhere that it was well over fifty and then wondered how many of them she'd seen. Cley Windmill was a very well-known landmark and even Agnes over the years had photographed it on many an occasion, although mainly from a nearby layby which was potentially a bit odd. Over the years, the windmill had been restored and was now holiday accommodation, so its future was secured and the magnificent sight that it was, would continue to be seen for generations to come and no doubt Agnes herself would continue to come and see it, and take the same photograph from the same layby for many years to come.

Pushing on with the road trip, Agnes motored through Blakeney, Wells-next-the-Sea and Holkham pausing only to ask herself why in all these years she'd never been to Holkham Hall. It always looked such a lovely place to visit and the Christmas events they held each year now were amazing. Maybe if there was time this year, she'd fit in a visit but if not, would a hundred percent be putting it in the diary for next year.

There was one final stop-off, not planned but suddenly urgently needed. After three hot chocolates, the bladder came calling: swiftly and urgently. Agnes knew the Clifftop car park in Old Hunstanton had public toilets which she very much hoped were open for a quick and potentially critical detour. In summers gone by, Agnes would be here with her cold chicken salad to picnic with, sat in the car overlooking the wide sandy beach below, and the memory led to a mental note for her to visit again in the warmer months with said salad in tow.

With a now calm bladder and no more hot chocolate allowed, Agnes set off for her final destination. It didn't take long to get there and although the public car park was open, the rest of the attraction was closed. This didn't matter though as Agnes had no plans to go in. She sat in the car looking round at the mainly empty parking bays; there were a few recreational walkers about and a couple of people with dogs on leads enjoying the fresh air but little else happening. Agnes knew she didn't need to be here for long, so she paid for just an hour's parking. Once the ticket had been safely put on the dashboard, Agnes set off to complete what she had come here to do. She walked along the path that led away from the car park, nodding and giving a brief hello to any passers-by whilst stopping and looking directly into each CCTV camera that lined the route. Most of the cameras were easy to spot but Agnes could also work out where the hidden ones were (she found one here once disguised as a duck, and then found a bench with a listening device located under the memorial plaque). Very slowly and deliberately, Agnes also made sure to look into the hidden cameras knowing that if she was right, the 'who' would certainly see her. And if she was wrong, well, that would be an interesting conversation with the police. After staring into seventeen cameras, Agnes decided that she'd done enough to get noticed and made her way back to the car for the journey home. She was now so cold, she could no longer feel her toes or fingertips, so setting the heater to maximum full blast volcanic heat she set off wondering what the 'who' would do next.

*

In an office at the 'where', the 'who' had a security alert pop up. Flicking on the CCTV images, the 'who' saw Agnes calmly and deliberately walk along the public access path, look up and into the cameras (visible and hidden). The 'who' smiled and a gave a brief nod of the head.

"Oh well done," the 'who' whispered, even though there was no one else in the room. "Nicely played."

Six

Still 4th December 2021

Delores was correct. Ellen didn't come back straight away about access to the factory, but she did dart into the bakery early on Saturday to see Agnes and let her know that she'd meet her and Delores in the car park at 11:00a.m. on Sunday. She'd have to leave them to it though, as they were having a family Sunday lunch out at a local pub, but she'd collect the keys off Agnes later that evening. Agnes decided this actually worked out quite well as it meant she'd be able to join the socially distanced Christmas Carols on the Beach event and the village Lantern Parade on Saturday evening after all. With a plan hatched, Ellen left the bakery carrying a pile of mince pies, three sourdough loaves, a baguette and two large apple pies, whilst ordering at the same time a Twelfth Night cake for four.

Agnes called Delores and left a message to confirm Sunday's arrangement and also to let her know that she was planning to be in the detective agency office for a few hours later that afternoon, going over the factory floor plans.

Delores saw her mobile phone ring but couldn't answer at the time as she was with a new client, although Delores couldn't help but wish she was an ex-client. Every suggestion Delores made was met with a 'no', or a 'not that' or 'I don't like that' and sometimes a definite 'absolutely not'. The client wanted a headpiece to match her outfit for a society wedding in the spring when big weddings were allowed again, but whilst she wanted it to match, she didn't want it to match too much. And then she wanted it to be discreet, yet a statement piece. Traditional in design, yet bold. Bespoke, but cheap. Delores could feel her nostrils adopt the beginning-to-flare pose as she muttered under her breath, "Do you also want it to play a tune?"

"What was that?" sniped the client.

"I said, do you need it soon?" replied Delores. Her client scowled a little before saying, "I don't think you're quite what I had in mind. You just don't get my vision," before getting up and marching out. Delores took some deep breaths in and out then stuck some pins in her stress doll as she listened to Agnes's message.

Agnes had the factory floor plans printed out and spread over one of the agency desks. It was a fairly straight forward layout. The factory was just off a busy road on the Harfreys Industrial Estate just outside Yarmouth. There was an easy access car park for staff and visitors, then what Agnes hoped was a slightly more secure gate leading to the transport yard and goods in/despatch areas. The factory and offices were all in the same building, offices at the front and the factory at the back. It wasn't the largest of operations, so with any luck she and Delores could do what they needed to in just a few hours on Sunday.

Agnes looked up as the entrance camera tingled and she saw Delores approach. Judging by the look on Delores's face, a plate of triple chocolate cookies was in desperate need. As Delores made her entrance, she threw her bag onto her desk. Failing to take into account how heavy said bag was, they both stopped and stared at the bag as it seemed to accelerate with speed as it slid at an impressive pace along the desk. Maintaining its trajectory, the bag knocked off a desk lamp, a pen tidy, a mouse, a tin of tea bags and with Agnes just catching it in time, Delores's favourite water glass as it hurtled towards the floor.

"Have you ever regretted your life choices?" Delores asked Agnes.

"Frequently," said Agnes. "Like that time I got salt and sugar mixed up." Agnes shuddered. "Trust me, Salted Strawberry Jam will never be the next big flavour sensation. Tough morning?" she asked Delores.

"The worst client from hell," said Delores. "Decided she wanted white accessories on a hat she'll be wearing to a wedding but wanted a very particular shade of white. I went through each and every shade I could get hold of... white... off white... bright white... barely white... shades of white... light white... pearlescent white... metallic white... hints of white... pearl white... but no. None of them were good enough. All I can say is that I hope I never see her again."

"She sounds like the wedding guest from hell," said Agnes. "Maybe the bride and groom will end up regretting inviting her."

"Doubt it," said Delores, "I don't think they've got much choice."

"Why?" asked Agnes.

"She's the vicar doing the service."

"Oh," said Agnes. "…Oh dear."

"Quite. Anyway, enough of the heavenly client from hell, any luck with the plans for tomorrow?"

"It's a four-part plan," said Agnes. "A look round the staff car park, then the offices, factory and finally the outside despatch bays. I want to see what can be seen, if you like, at Ground Zero, understand the environment and how easy or hard it would be for someone to gain access."

"Are we looking for anything in particular?" asked Delores.

"No, I don't think so," said Agnes. "I guess we'll know if we see it, but we won't know unless we see it, so we'll have to see it to know it."

"Well, that makes total sense," said Delores who was gradually calming down after her trying morning. She took another cookie from the plate but both her and Agnes's attention was diverted to the security camera as it began to tingle again. They were surprised though as it wasn't the normal entrance camera but the discreet side entrance to the agency. Delores looked perplexed. "Were we expecting anyone today?"

Agnes shook her head. "No, not today, and most certainly *not* from that entrance."

"Maybe they're lost," said Delores.

"It's quite a specific well-hidden entrance to say the least," said Agnes. "It's not really somewhere you can drive by and get lost by accident."

They carried on watching the monitors and saw a

dark, very big, very expensive Jaguar pull up. The driver's door opened, and a smart, well-dressed chauffeur got out. He turned, almost glided to the rear passenger door and opened it. An equally smartly dressed, very distinguished older gentleman exited the vehicle, about six foot two, hair mainly grey, cut so short it screamed ex-military. Trousers with creases so sharp you'd cut your finger if you touched them. The man looked briefly around before staring into the camera that was rigidly and purposely trained on him. Delores still looked perplexed but as Agnes stared back at the man staring into the camera, she suddenly gave a slight, almost unnoticeable smile. "Well, well, well," she said quietly to herself. Delores looked over at her.

"Come on," said Agnes, making her way down to the agency entrance side door.

Delores followed Agnes down, but she was still unsure of the man and what they were about to open the door to, so she picked up a stash of felt-board pins and Agnes's trusty stapler, just in case. She also couldn't help but think— *oval-shaped face, head on the large size, maybe twenty-four inches round... silk top hat with pale blue silk lining.* She snapped out of it though when she heard Agnes yell, "Come on, Delores!"

Upon opening the secure door, they saw that the visitor was even more distinguished in reality, well-polished shiny shoes and most definitely wearing a made-to-measure bespoke tailored suit. The visitor looked at both of them before saying, "Good afternoon, ladies," in a very well-spoken voice.

"Afternoon," said Agnes and Delores at the same time.

"I take it you were expecting me," he said.

"No," said Delores.

"Oh yes," said Agnes which made Delores look round at her.

"Maybe you should invite me in, and we can discuss things further," the man said.

"No." said Delores.

"Oh yes," said Agnes. Delores looked back at Agnes then over at the man. The man looked straight back at Delores.

"You have no idea who I am, do you?" he said to her.

"No idea whatsoever," said Delores, reaching in her pocket for a defensive pin. The man looked at Agnes.

"But I suspect you do."

"Oh yes," said Agnes again. Delores now at peak puzzlement once more looked at Agnes. Agnes looked back at Delores.

"This is Armadillo."

With military precision Armadillo suddenly took the lead and charged his way up to the office. Delores leant over to Agnes and said, "You sweep for bugs right?"

"More often than you realise," replied Agnes, but making a mental note to sweep inside, outside, the bakery, the millinery workshop and their respective cars as soon as Armadillo had left.

When they were seated in the office, with customary tea and biscuits duly offered and accepted (Agnes taking every opportunity to add to her fingerprint collection), and crisps from Crispin Crisps respectfully declined, Armadillo began.

"Please accept my sincere apologies for the circumstances of my arrival and prior exploratory checks.

I needed to be entirely certain of your backgrounds and suitability for a rather discreet task you are required to complete."

Delores was in the main still very confused and very glad she had her hat pins still close to hand if needed.

Armadillo noted Delores's confused look.

"I take it you still have no idea who I am?" he said to her.

"Nope, no idea whatsoever," she replied.

"But you do?" Armadillo said in the direction of Agnes.

"Yes, I do. But I only know *you're* the 'who', because of your arrival today. Once I figured out *where* the 'where' was, the 'who' could have been anyone, so I did some further research."

"For those of us in a state of fugue and liable to lose our wahoolies at any given moment," said Delores, nostrils on flare standby, "could one of you please speak in plain English and please explain what on God's green earth is happening right now?" As she finished speaking Delores had a feeling of horror come over her. Was how she was feeling now, how Monsieur Delvene felt when he had no idea what she was going on about when she was trying to explain her latest concept to him? Did this moment explain his quizzical looks, raised eyebrow and degrees of increasingly hard to understand French accent?

"Delores… Delores…" said Agnes, trying and failing to bring Delores back into the here and now. Delores remained zoned out. Agnes tried another tack. "I've stapled the hem on my skirt back up."

"You've done *what*?" cried Delores. "Step away from the stapler, it's too much!"

"Thought that would do it," said Agnes. "Are you back in the present with us?"

"What? Yes… back… carry on… obvs not with the stapler though."

"Perhaps I should explain," said Armadillo.

"Probably best," said Delores.

Armadillo began.

"My name is Francis, Earl Culperston, but I'm also known as Lord Bacham," (pronounced Beecham) "of Bacham." Delores frowned; she knew she'd heard this name somewhere before but couldn't quite place it.

"Maybe, Ms Marshall, you know me by my job title."

"Which is?" asked Delores.

"Lord Chamberlain to the Sovereign, currently based in Norfolk."

"Oh…" said Delores, the mists clearing. "*Oh!*… So the '*where*' is…"

"Yes," said Agnes, "the '*where*' is absolutely '*there*'."

"Okay," said Delores, "that clears up the 'who' and 'where' but not the 'why' or 'what'. *Why* did you try and access our data, *what* do you want from us and *why* Armadillo?"

"I'm entirely with Delores on this one," said Agnes. "Two whys and a what please."

"Your reputation with this agency is well known in certain circles," said Armadillo. "Your additional collaboration with the Women's Club in Norfolk does of course include several members of the family and one in particular likes to be kept in the loop, as it were, by the group leader. As such, you and what you do is well known to many who work within certain circles in certain walls."

"So that means you also know about certain headpieces worn by certain people to certain events and garden parties," said Delores.

"Absolutely," said Armadillo, "the family like to be of assistance when needed so understand that some of your ladies have all manner of decor in their headwear, some of which may disguise a camera or a listening device. Of course, the family would never put themselves in such a position where they are directly implicated but they are well aware that nervous chatter around them can reveal far more than intended."

"Okay," said Delores, "but what about the first 'why'? Why did you try and access our data?"

"For the simple reason to ensure you are as good as your reputation," was Armadillo's swift reply, "and clearly you are as it was impossible to get through your security. In fact, I've not seen such levels of encryption since the new system was installed in the Security Services."

Agnes looked very pleased with herself. She smiled and nodded whilst deeply hoping and praying that Armadillo didn't ask how she was able to access such secure data protection software.

"One 'why' down," Agnes said. "What about the second? Why 'Armadillo'?"

"Maybe we should do the *what* first," replied Armadillo, "as it will explain the *why*."

"Go on," said Delores.

Armadillo took a breath and began.

"What we... *I*... would like, is your help. A document

has gone missing, call it a ledger to be more precise, and we need you to help recover it. At this stage we don't know if it was maliciously taken or removed by accident and because of that, and because of its contents, we need to keep this off the record, as it were. Whether malicious or by accident we also have no idea if the person or people who took the ledger fully understand the contents or what they'd do with the information should they work out exactly what it is they've got. Suffice to say this ledger goes to the heart of the family and would be deeply damaging should the contents be revealed. Put simply, I need you to find the ledger and return it to me and only me."

"Can you tell us what's inside the ledger?" asked Delores.

"No," replied Armadillo.

"When did it go missing?" asked Agnes.

"We don't know," said Armadillo.

"Where was it taken from?" asked Delores.

"We don't know," said Armadillo.

"And yet you want us to find it?" asked Agnes.

"Yes," said Armadillo.

"And you actually think we can find it, with pretty much no information?" asked Delores.

"Yes," said Armadillo again. "What I can tell you is that the ledger was last seen in Norfolk a month ago when the family arrived for a long weekend. When they left, it was discovered that a number of items had gone missing including some silver from my outer office. My deputy notified me immediately but had assumed that as the ledger was normally kept in my inner office that it would have gone to Aberdeenshire with me, however when I realised it was not in my box, the alarm bells started to ring... although silently. The family were only in residence briefly before some left for Cornwall and some to Aberdeenshire.

"If this ledger is so important, you'd think the family would take better care of it," said Delores.

"They don't know about the ledger, so that would make it rather difficult," said Armadillo.

Agnes and Delores looked at one another, amazed.

"What do you mean they don't know about the ledger? You've just said it goes to the heart of the family. How can they not know about it?" said Agnes.

"Forgive me, but again it's not something I can tell you. But I can assure you, it does go to the heart of the family and it's absolutely vital that the ledger is found and returned to me, as soon as possible."

"But you've also said that it was discovered missing a month ago," said Agnes. "Why wait so long to contact us?"

"I needed some time to conduct my own search," said Armadillo, "but it became obvious that this was causing some day-to-day difficulties. To calm those at the top of the family and allay any fears of a burglary, I told them it was internal procedural incident testing and that my team and I had made a brief report to the police of the missing items as part of the test. However the ledger was not mentioned to the family or the police. I then conducted a review of your agency and your skills leading to where we are today."

"I also don't understand though," said Delores, "if this ledger 'at the heart of the family' is so important why don't they know about it and why come to outsiders to find it?"

Armadillo looked at Delores.

"The ledger is an historical document passed down to each Lord Chamberlain in role as Protector in Chief. Please believe me when I say that the ledger going missing whilst under my protection is profoundly embarrassing and in any other circumstances I would resign my position, but circumstances which I cannot share with you forbid me from doing so. As to why outsiders… you are renowned in your work and reputation and are known to the family, so whilst they will never know of your assistance, they would command me to thank you for your impending work to retrieve it." Delores remained unconvinced and was about to voice her objection, but Armadillo continued. "And because I don't know if someone internally or externally took it. If internally, was it an accident or was it malicious and by whom and why? If external, how did someone gain access to the private apartments without being caught? And yes, you're right, normally there are secure internal channels who would deal with these situations, but as they aren't aware of the ledger and its contents, I'd rather keep this external with you for the time being. As for the other items that are missing, we filed a low-level report with the Norfolk police; they came in and took some details but were intentionally not told the entire truth. The incident therefore was lodged as a 'procedural test', so the view is that it was an operational exercise and nothing to pursue." Armadillo paused. "Trust me, a great deal of research has been done into what you do in this detective agency, and you have been very carefully selected."

"What details did the police take?" asked Agnes.

"Some photographs and statements from some of the staff. I never asked to see the report as I didn't want the police to think there was actually anything in it."

"And what were the other items that had gone missing?"

"An eighteenth-century silver cow creamer, two gold candlesticks, several first-edition books and a hand-weaved Welsh woollen blanket."

"Any of it valuable?"

"That depends on your interpretation of valuable," said Armadillo. "Several thousand pounds for the jug, around £2,000 for the candlesticks, maybe £1,000 on the books and as for the blanket, commercially of no value but sentimentally irreplaceable."

"We can definitely get the ladies into Norfolk Constabulary to have a look at the file, just to see if there is anything that may help," said Agnes. "Was it Wymondham station?"

"Correct," said Armadillo.

"So you can't tell us what's in the ledger. You can't tell us when it was taken. You can't tell us where it was taken, so how exactly do you think we're going to find it?" asked Delores.

Armadillo looked at her. "That, my dear, is down to your ingenuity and creativeness. I have no doubt you'll come up with something."

"What about access to these places?" said Agnes. "It sounds like we'll need to get our people into the Norfolk, Cornwall and Aberdeenshire properties. We can send in the ladies for their "normal" day trips and can brief them on their next get-together. But I imagine behind-the-scenes access will be slightly harder to get. Can I take it for granted that if there are any suitable jobs our team could do, you'll ensure they're successful?"

Armadillo nodded. "That won't be a problem. All I'll need is their names and the jobs applied for."

"Well, I guess that's a start," said Agnes. "Can you at least tell us though, what the ledger looks like?"

"That's one thing I can tell you," said Armadillo. "It's approximately the size of an A5 notebook in a leather-bound case. It looks like a reading book. On the front it simply says, 'Property of the Lord Chamberlain.'"

"And what about who was in the house at the time, or at least the last time you saw it?" asked Delores.

"I can provide this information as well," said Armadillo, "as well as where each person went when they left Norfolk."

Delores looked at Agnes.

"Well, we've found cats with less information. I didn't think anything could top rummaging through the undergrowth, shouting out 'Warlord, Warlord, where are you?' with a pack of cat treats in my hand, but sounds like this will top it."

Armadillo smiled. "As I said, ingenuity and creativeness."

"What about the last *why*?" asked Agnes.

"Why Armadillo?"

"An armadillo wears its armour on the outside. Tough, impenetrable and when under attack can entirely protect itself... the shell protecting what's important on the inside. That's what I do. I am the armour on the outside protecting the family on the inside."

"Can we call you by your actual name?" asked Delores. "It seems a bit weird to keep calling you by the name of a small, strange-looking mammal."

"For now, let's keep with Armadillo," said the Lord Chamberlain, "in the spirit of the animal protecting what's important by keeping identities secret."

"Fair enough," said Delores, whilst still under the certain belief that this was all just a bit 'odd'.

And with that, Armadillo was gone, promising to provide Agnes and Delores with the information that he was able to share the next day.

"Do you believe him?" asked Delores to Agnes.

"He's definitely who he says he is, and he definitely works where he says he does," said Agnes. "As for what he wants us to find, a document so important that he's the only one who knows about it, I'm not sure. But, it'll be interesting to find out."

"Sure will," said Delores. "Now, in the meantime, if you can do your thing and sweep this place for bugs and anything else dodgy, I'll start to think of a way to get the ladies onto the mission. I'm thinking tea towels."

Agnes looked at Delores.

"Tea towels?"

Delores nodded. "Yep, tea towels."

"...And you think I'm weird," said Agnes.

Seven

Sunday, 5th December 2021

Sunday came round as it usually did after a Saturday, and this particular Sunday found Agnes and Delores waiting in the factory car park for Ellen. The factory car park was empty so neither had any parking difficulties, well, apart from Delores and her attempts to reverse into an empty space, surrounded by empty spaces at the furthest point of the empty car park from the entrance. Fortunately, the hedge took the worst of it and as Delores told herself, 'it'll grow back'.

Agnes had a different parking issue; she always reversed into a space, even if it was surrounded by empty spaces as she found it easier to drive in reverse than going forward (even when not parking she found driving in reverse easier). She wasn't entirely convinced this was the ideal way to drive but also decided it was probably safer not to tell anyone this.

Whilst they were waiting for Ellen, they wandered round the grounds of the factory. As per the floor plans that Agnes had printed off a few days back, the main reception and offices were at the front and the factory was attached to the back. From the outside, the office area matched the plans and wasn't that big so Agnes remained confident they could quickly get done what they needed. With any luck the inside layout of the offices and factory would match just the same.

The staff car park was big, but not that big and at the back was a transport yard with bays for six lorries; three for goods in and three for despatch. Agnes made a note there was no CCTV covering the car park, reception entrance or the goods in and despatch bays. She wandered over to the car park entrance and looked up and down the road. It was a busy road right through the industrial estate; even on a Sunday there seemed to be a never-ending convoy of lorries traipsing along it. The main road was well lit and had the odd speed camera box here and there. Agnes wondered if there was a problem more with speeding cars along here as the road was very straight with good sight lines. She took a few pictures of some of the street furniture and the view to the left and right from the factory to help keep the image alive when they were back at the agency.

Agnes also noted, with some alarm, that not only was there no CCTV for the factory car park or transport bays, there also didn't appear to be any gates, or barriers or any security whatsoever to deter anyone from wandering in. The back of the transport bay backed onto a no-longer-used single-track lane with only some rough hedging acting as a separation. *It would be far too easy for someone to squeeze through here to access the factory*, she thought to herself. They were almost asking for trouble and based on why she and Delores were here, Crispin Crisps got what they asked for.

Delores walked the opposite way round to Agnes. She noted some litter in the hedging, a smoking shelter with a very full cigarette bin… would it be too disgusting to remove some of the stubbed-out cigarettes to add to the DNA collection? She decided it would and aside from that, she knew there wasn't enough anti-bac gel or bleach in the world (well, okay her car) to clean down afterwards.

Delores heard some voices near the car park entrance and for a moment wondered if Ellen had arrived. She glanced up but saw it wasn't Ellen and saw instead some workers on a stroll from a nearby factory. Always up for a chat (and an opportunity to sell someone a hat), Delores wandered over to the group. After introductions were made, Delores went with an explanation of being there ahead of Monday's Christmas bazaar to see how much room they'd have in the car park for display materials. She stayed chatting to the group for about five minutes and when Agnes turned round to call her over to look at something, she saw Delores seemingly sewing something onto a jacket. *Well, that's not at all odd*, thought Agnes, *but there again it's Delores so anything's possible.*

When her chat with her new friends had finished, Delores didn't immediately walk back into the factory car park. Instead she crossed the road and looked up at something that her new friends had pointed out to her and then came back into the car park.

"Anything interesting?" she called out to Agnes.

"Interesting, horrifying and intriguing," replied Agnes. "What about you, and were you *actually* sewing just then?"

"Absolutely," said Delores. "That was Andrew, he had a loose button on his jacket, so I offered to whip it off and sew it back on for him."

"Andrew...?" said Agnes. "I didn't know you knew anyone who worked round here."

"Oh I don't," said Delores, "but the old emergency sewing kit in the bag is an absolute boon in getting someone to stay longer to talk to me. Nice little chat we had and possibly a sale as well as his brother didn't know what to get his son for Christmas, so I suggested a bespoke flat cap; he can bring the child in and let him choose his own colour and style. All round result!"

"Tremendous," said Agnes. "What about anything useful for the investigation?"

"Oh yes, lots of information," said Delores. "Did you know that Charlie..." But she stopped speaking as Ellen at that moment pulled into the car park. "Tell you back at the agency," Delores said quickly to Agnes.

Ellen drove in and pulled up alongside where Agnes and Delores were standing. She smiled if a little hesitantly knowing why they were both here and what she was asking them to find out.

"Morning, both," she called out. "Chilly one today." Agnes and Delores nodded their heads in agreement.

"How are you, Ellen?" asked Delores.

"I'm telling myself this is the right thing to be doing to get to the bottom of this mystery once and for all."

"Even if your worst fear is confirmed?"

"Even if my worst fear is confirmed. I've got no choice, Delores."

"Well, let's see what we find first," said Agnes. "We've

got a list of things to look at when we're inside so hopefully we'll be several steps closer to finding out what's going on for you. Oh and I brought some additional masks, aprons and hair nets from my bakery for when we go round the factory to keep everything clean."

"Thank you," said Ellen handing over the keys. "The production staff always start with a thorough clean before each shift but don't worry, I trust you. Now, this is the key to get in via the reception doors and I've added a sticker on each of the other keys, so you know which key is for which office and which are for the factory areas."

"Are you still okay to come and collect the keys later?" asked Agnes. "I can text you when we're done here and then I'll be in the bakery until very, very late so whatever works for you."

"That's fine, I'll be able to pop out for about twenty minutes so no one will notice when I come and collect them. Also I've got something for you in the back of my car. Hang on two ticks and I'll get it for you."

"Lovely," said Agnes, although hoping very much it wasn't more crisps, "and are we still on to attend the Christmas bazaar tomorrow? We've got the ladies lined up for tea and biscuits."

"Yes, all good for tomorrow. We've got a few local businesses attending so you'll fit in quite nicely." Ellen handed over two large black bags to Agnes, the bags making an ominous crinkling sound like a bag of crisps. Agnes peered into the bags and raised her eyebrows.

"Oh okay, thank you. These could be very useful," she said before walking over to her car to chuck the black bags in the boot.

"Hopefully tomorrow will go well for you and the other businesses. I think everyone could do with some normality," said Delores. "Oh and, Ellen, it may just be me, but what's that smell round here? It's quite… pungent…"

Ellen sniffed. "Cheese and Onion I think."

And with this the goodbyes were said giving Ellen enough time to get to her family lunch and for Delores and Agnes to begin the search.

"Do we need another wander around the car park," asked Delores, "or are you happy to make a start inside?"

"Let's go inside. We've both had a walk round out here and we can do another one if needed when we leave but let's make a start on the inside."

"Fine with me," said Delores, looking forward to getting out of the chilly Cheese and Onion December air.

Agnes pushed the key into the lock and turned it with ease.

"The lack of security in this place makes me weep," she said.

"But on the plus side, we can get in and have a hunt round and no one apart from Ellen will be any the wiser," replied Delores.

The factory reception had a seating area to the left with the reception desk immediately in front. There were doors just beyond the desk taking you left or right and straight ahead were stairs going up.

Delores looked at the plans.

"Based on this we've got Finance, Legal, IT and HR to the right, Supply Chain, Marketing, Product and Operations to the left. Upstairs is the canteen, some larger meeting rooms and the directors' offices and seriously, that Cheese and Onion smell is getting stronger."

"I know," said Agnes. "I'm not sure if it's making me feel hungry or faint."

"Well let's hope it's hunger, because if you faint, you're on your own. I'm out of here."

"In that case, probably best we start then and let's go right to finance. That was the start of the sabotage so let's start at the start."

"Sounds like a plan."

Finance, Legal, HR and IT all sat in one open-plan office, with the IT server room to one side. Each division was marked by different coloured columns and a department sign hanging from the ceiling to denote each team. There were two small meeting rooms in the same space but in the main, the office looked very similar to all other modern open-plan offices: desks in groups of four, each desk with at least one monitor, a desk phone, filing tray and a set of drawers underneath. Despite posters on the wall promoting a clear-desk policy, most desks had used mugs on them containing an indeterminable brown liquid and the 'paperless' office was anything but.

Delores and Agnes, both by this time wearing protective gloves, went round to each desk and carefully and methodically went through any paperwork left on the desks or in unlocked drawers and they rooted through unlocked filing cabinets. There wasn't anything that stood out. There was the odd desk where clearly the occupier was the stationery hoarder, the sweet supplier (maybe the sweets offset the crisps and the ever stronger odour of cheese and onion), the minimalist desk occupier and the ram-everything-in-the-drawers-because-someone-will-ask-for-something-one-day desk occupier.

Whilst Delores was busy lifting fingerprints from desks, Agnes tried her luck at each of the computers. Some people were laptop users who'd taken their laptop home, but some had left their laptops plugged in at their desk. Agnes always found this strange… surely the whole point of a laptop was that it was portable so you could take it home with you at the end of the day, otherwise what was the point of one? Most desktop computers were switched off but far too many people had notepads on their desks or in their drawers with a page of passwords written down and helpfully next to each password the program it was for.

Working as quickly as she could, she logged on to each computer and had a quick look round any stored documents and emails. Judging by some of the email conversations it was clear there were several unhappy groups of employees, and some had clearly applied for roles elsewhere, but nothing so far to link back to any of the leaks. Agnes made a mental note to remind Ellen that it might be a good idea to remind employees never to put anything on a company email that you wouldn't want your boss to read. Or anyone who wasn't the intended recipient. Or IT. Didn't the employees realise that every email went through the company's internal servers?

Thinking of IT, Agnes went next to the server room. It was a small office just behind the IT desks, although calling it an office was probably stretching the truth somewhat. It was more cupboard than office.

Agnes let herself into the server room taking no notice

whatsoever of the RESTRICTED ACCESS sign above the (unlocked) door. She thought if they really meant restricted access, then the door would actually have been locked, but then based on what they'd found so far in their search, IT would probably hang the key on the wall next to the door.

The server room was more of a glorified cupboard than an office, with some racking on one side, piled to the brim with laptop bits, spare parts for desk phones and random cables that no one knew connected to what anymore but were kept just in case. There weren't any windows in the room but there was an air-con unit doing its best to keep the room cool and counteract the heat coming from the machines. There was also a light bulb, a single chocolate from a selection box and one sock on the floor underneath the desk. *Well, at least it isn't underpants,* thought, Agnes.

Agnes pulled out her trusty tablet and connected it to the machines running each of the servers and began downloading data. When she got to about seventy percent she almost jumped out of her skin when Delores put her head round the door and asked, "Found anything?"

"Jeez, you scared me!"

"Sorry, didn't mean to. I'm done going through everything on this side so just wondering how you're getting on," said Delores.

"Almost done," said Agnes. "I can look at this data on here..." – pointing to her tablet – "...when I'm back at the agency, but so far nothing's jumping out. How about you?"

"Nothing hugely significant, although it's interesting that none of the Secret Santa victims work on this side, but there does appear to be a lot of unhappy people working here and I don't think Ellen or Charles has any clue as to how they're feeling. Even Richard, the HR director has got a job application for a company in Wales printed off on his desk; he doesn't seem to have made any attempt to hide it. But then he's also got a 'lucky unicorn' decoration hanging from his monitor so I'm not entirely certain of his wellbeing at the moment."

"Sounds like our list of suspects may have got a bit bigger then."

"Possibly, possibly not. All I can really see are unhappy words not actions," said Delores, "so no one's causing any red flags to start waving."

"But that's how this all started – unhappy words on an email," replied Agnes, looking at her tablet when it bleeped to confirm the download was complete. "Okay, that's this downloaded. Shall we move onto the next lot of desks? I think you said Supply Chain, Marketing, Product and Operations?"

Delores nodded. "Yep, they're on the other side of this floor." Agnes nodded as she removed her data cable from the server. Giving the room one last check over to make sure they hadn't left anything, they both left for the other open-plan office to perform the same searches.

This side of the building was an identikit layout of where they'd just come from... desks in groups of four, each desk with at least one monitor, a desk phone, filing tray and a set of drawers underneath and the same posters on the walls. The only reason for knowing it was different was purely the signs with the team names on.

"It's either comfortably reassuringly the same so you

feel you belong or it's unimaginative corporateness," said Delores.

"The latter I feel," replied Agnes looking round.

"But," said Delores, "we do have a Secret Santa victim on this side of the building." She glanced down at her notes. "Alice Alderman, a senior operations manager."

"Ahh yes," said Agnes, "the itching powder."

"That's the one; two directors, two in Transport, one Factory Manager and one in Operations. But it's only Alice on this entire ground floor who was a victim."

"Let's take a really close look at the contents of her desk and if she's got a desktop computer I'll get as much as I can from it. Weird isn't it though, three people essentially in corporate-style roles and three in warehouse jobs?"

"Could be deliberately even, or deliberately targeted. I'm not sure we can call it either way just yet."

"Agreed, but let's see what I can pull off from the servers and tomorrow if you and the ladies take the lead chatting to everyone, we might find the missing link."

Delores nodded and added, "Although I very much hope by tomorrow the smell of cheese and onion has well and truly gone."

"Maybe that's what caused the perpetrator to go rogue... the smell!" said Agnes.

Repeating the same actions as before, Agnes went round all desks and where there were desktops or left-behind laptops she logged in and swept through the data. Delores lifted as many prints as she could and rifled... carefully rifled... through any files that were lying around or in unlocked cupboards.

Paying particular attention to Alice's desk, Delores

found a diary with the 19th of January circled in red and the letters 'CC' in the circle.

"Now that's interesting," she muttered, checking her phone to look at the timelines. The 19th of January was when the email came in from the bank with their concerns re the loan Crispin Crisps wanted. And CC, well that was Charles's brother, Crispin Crispin, Director of Marketing and Brand who happened to be who Alice reported into. Flicking through the months, Delores also found the 8th of April circled in red again and once more 'CC'. "Curiouser and curiouser," she muttered, for the 9th of April was when HMRC came calling.

Delores called Agnes over and showed her what she'd found.

"Well, well, well," said Agnes. "Now that is very interesting."

"Affair?" asked Delores.

"Could be," said Agnes. "I'll compare both their diaries and bank statements… see if anything links them further."

"What about mobile phone records?"

"Those as well but bearing in mind any contact in the working day could be reasonably explained. Even out of hours… well, she reports into him and it's not unknown for there to be contact in teams or with your manager outside of office hours. But that's no reason to discount it; it's more of a reason to look a bit closer."

"Maybe CC was jealous that as the younger brother he didn't inherit the business and it went to Charles as the oldest. CC would have access to all the company information so he could have got Alice to leak it."

"It's definitely a possibility," said Agnes. "Family

dynamics can be a nightmare at the best of times, but a family-run business? That's a million types of chaos."

"Or at least six," said Delores. "After all, Secret Santa slayed six. Charles and Alice were victims, so was it linked to CC?"

"But then why Charles and not CC? I agree the message on the jigsaw 'I know what you did' could apply far more to CC than Charles, so why wasn't CC a victim?"

"Mistaken identity," said Delores. "After all, both their initials are CC."

"But so are Charlie's," said Agnes, "Charles Crispin, Crispin Crispin and Charlie Crispin – all have the initials CC."

"Now that is a good point," said Delores. "More to check when we do the directors' offices upstairs."

Agnes nodded, her mind whizzing with possibilities.

It wasn't too long until the search of this side of the ground floor was also complete, so Agnes and Delores made their way up to the first floor. At the top of the stairs were the doors to the canteen which had the factory underneath it and to the left and right were all the directors' offices, two large meeting rooms and a couple of smaller rooms. Although the directors had offices, they were simply glass partitioned with blinds for privacy when needed and wooden doors. Charles had the biggest office space and there was a smaller partition just in front which his PA used. Clearly no one got to Charles without Anne Mayhew knowing or letting them pass. Like most directors with PAs, it was the PA who actually had the seat of power and total control of what was going on.

"Canteen first?" asked Delores.

Agnes nodded and followed Delores in. It was a decent-sized place; to one side was the kitchen and serving bays and on the other, tables and chairs which had all been spaced out to give the staff plenty of socially distanced room. There was a TV, a newspaper and book stand, a bulletin board and box upon box of Crispin Crisps for the staff to help themselves to. The canteen had been decorated with several Christmas trees, twinkling lights, reindeer, snowflakes and Santa ornaments.

"Look," said Delores, "we found Santa!"

Unfortunately, the downside to the canteen being over the factory was that the cheese and onion smell was now at maximum on the scale of strong, unpleasant odours.

"Don't get me wrong," said Agnes, "I very much enjoy a cheese and onion crisp, several in fact... many many crisps... the more crisps the merrier... but that smell is enough to drive even me to insanity. I think *I'd* start committing crimes if I had to inhale that every day."

"Maybe they get used to it," said Delores, frantically resisting the urge to gag. "Nose blindness, I think it's called."

"Revolting is what it is," said Agnes. "Revolting. So let's get the search done in here as quickly as possible. I can't image we'll find much, so let's get it over and done with and move to the offices as soon as humanly possible."

Agnes took the kitchen and Delores the staff seating area. There weren't any computers or IT equipment in either place so that made the search quicker. Delores tried to get some prints from the tables and chairs but there were just too many and most were smudged so in the end she gave up. In the kitchen Agnes found all the right

Health and Safety protocols were being followed and she even checked the ingredients cupboard. The contents of jars and bottles did indeed match the labels. *No flavouring mix up here,* Agnes thought to herself.

Agnes stuck her head through the swing doors that separated the kitchen from the serving and seating areas.

"Anything?" she called out.

"Nope," said Delores, "you?"

"Nothing."

"Offices next?" asked Agnes.

"Yep," said Delores, desperate to get out of the cheese and onion smell. "Crisp?" She motioned towards the boxes upon boxes of freebie crisps on offer.

"Well I might just have a couple," said Agnes wandering over and reaching for her favourite.

"Seriously?" said Delores. "You still pick Cheese and Onion, even with this smell around us?"

"Glutton for punishment," said Agnes watching Delores make her selection. "Anyway, good luck with your Prawn Cocktail ones… hope they don't turn out to be Cajun Squirrel."

Delores considered the probabilities of this being the case and decided to swap her crisp selection for Ready Salted although with a deep-filled fear and dread that they might turn out to be Marmite flavour instead.

They left the canteen and reviewed the office space; all the directors had their offices up here.

"It's a bit 'us and them', isn't it?" said Delores.

"Agreed," said Agnes. "Not really the way to harbour positive employee relations. But let's check every office thoroughly, after all two of the victims are based up here." Working their way through each office, they repeated the same searches as downstairs. Any desk which still had a laptop or desktop on it was fired up and a sweep done of any documents stored and emails sent. Agnes was always amazed but quite relieved to see that most people didn't clear out their Drafts, Sent or Bin folders so she was able to easily and quickly copy the contents.

Agnes could see very quickly that Charlie had been researching automation and AI in the workplace and he was clearly planning some very big changes when his time came to inherit the business. His deleted web history showed day after day all the pages he'd looked at as well as financial websites on how to become more profitable. Agnes thought about her own little bakery and how much joy it gave her knowing that everything she sold had been made either by her or her staff by hand with love. She knew that in a large-scale production factory there had to be machinery and automation but by ditching the human touch surely your product just became another soulless product on a shelf. Maybe this didn't matter to Charlie if it kept the money flowing in.

Charlie had a three-drawer unit under his desk, which of course was not locked. Going through the contents, Agnes found the usual things, chocolate bar wrappers, random pencils, Post-it notes, magazines (*Savoury Snack Monthly*), a single polo mint... and pushed in the middle of a 2020 diary, a piece of paper folded in half. She opened it up and had a read.

"Delores!" Agnes called out.

Delores came over to the office door. "You called?"

"Come and look at this." Delores came into Charlie's office and had a look at what Agnes was waving.

"Ohhh, that's interesting," said Delores. "Doesn't look good for Charlie, does it?"

"Not really," said Agnes. "This is a list of suppliers who had orders with them cancelled and over here is the list of suppliers who had payments cancelled. He's written 'Lizzie' next to them."

"So he causes the carnage knowing that this will humiliate Lizzie as Supply Chain Director," said Delores.

"And don't forget, Lizzie was also a Secret Santa victim," said Agnes.

"So now we have Alice, Charles and Lizzie who can be linked to the sabotage and Secret Santa," said Delores.

"It's beginning to very much look that way," said Agnes.

Delores left the office and went over to the line of filing cabinets alongside the wall. It seemed like every purchase order, invoice and contract had been kept for well over ten years. There were files detailing suppliers and large wholesale and retail customers... everything was here, and everything was easily available for anyone to access. There was even another cabinet full of finance information including bank statements and utility bills.

"Honestly," she said to Agnes, "it's like stepping back in time to a business from the 1990s. Everything is paper based, and everything is here for anyone to look through. They even still have a fax machine!"

"Maybe they thought that a paper trail was a way of avoiding hacking," said Agnes.

"Possibly," said Delores, "but even if they wanted to

avoid electronic hacking, they've left themselves wide open to physical hacking."

"Totally," said Agnes, "although what is very helpful is the list on Anne's desk with all the staff who put their names in the Secret Santa hat. At least we know exactly who to target first and with any luck we might see them tomorrow at the bazaar."

"Long live paper," said Delores.

Once the search of the office spaces had concluded, Agnes and Delores moved down to the factory area. They decided to go round the factory as if they were a potato on its transformation from tuber to crunchy-based snack. Somewhat strangely, in the factory, the cheese and onion smell was far less prominent than in the offices. Agnes and Delores paused to put on the protective gear Agnes had brought with her to avoid any cross-contamination in the food areas.

"Do you think the factory staff taunt the office staff and waft the smell up to them?" asked Delores. Agnes briefly envisaged all the factory staff holding up massive fans trying to shift the air and the aroma out of the factory and into the offices, but then decided that was too weird even for this factory.

"Let's just hope it's better ventilation in here," she said, "and enjoy the clean, fresh air."

Beginning their journey as a potato in the factory they started off at goods in. There were three bays for the deliveries and all bay doors were locked from the inside.

"Well, at least that's something," said Delores.

There was a large whiteboard next to the bay doors marked 'Monday to Friday' and 'AM and PM' with the number of incoming lorries booked in. There was then a tick box to confirm once the truck had come in and been unloaded. The whiteboard was already marked up with the following week's deliveries: potatoes, flavourings, oils and packaging. Everything and anything you'd need to make a crunchy-based snack.

Agnes took photos of the area and the whiteboard whilst Delores went through the desks. There was just one computer and one printer in this section, which made for a very quick search. As with the office space, Agnes and Delores weren't surprised that the factory still ran on paper. They wondered what would happen if the factory ever ran out of paper or ink, or if a printer stopped working. It made them wonder if some of Charlie's ideas were such a bad thing.

From goods in, Agnes and Delores, channelling their inner potato persona, moved next to the production area.

"Is it just me or are you doing a voiceover in your head telling the audience how a crisp is made?" asked Delores.

"Just you," said Agnes, but now hearing an inner voice saying, 'once unloaded, our triumphant tubers dance their merry way along the factory floor to get their skin off and their flavourings on'.

"Shush now," said Agnes to herself, "too loud, man, too loud."

"What was that?" asked Delores.

"Nothing!" said Agnes very quickly, her other inner voice telling the first inner voice to shush once more.

From what seemed a basic goods in area, the production lines started to get more mechanical and industrial. There was a large cauldron-esque-looking machine where the potatoes were washed – their first stage in their journey to becoming a crunchy-based snack.

"It's a big washing machine!" said Delores.

"But hopefully without the laundry detergent and fabric softener," said Agnes.

The potatoes then went on a conveyer belt along a line where actual human beings could then hook out any bad or poor-quality ones. The inner voice came back to Agnes… 'and look at those squeaky-clean, shower-fresh terrific tubers ready to go!'. Agnes shook her head as if she had water in her ears to try and stop the voice.

"Shush… stop it!" she shushed to herself.

Up next was the peeler and slicer and as both these machines had been tampered with additional attention was paid to them. The peeler was clearly loaded by hand, with the potatoes going into what looked like a big drum which clearly rotated. The drum had little spikes around its edge which clearly peeled the potatoes as they went round and round.

'Look at them go!' went the inner voice. 'Jiggling and bouncing round and round, getting more and more naked by the second… woah!!'.

"Now that's just daft," said Agnes to her inner voice.

Agnes and Delores studied the peeler in detail. It looked like the washed potatoes were put in big plastic crates, then lifted up and emptied into the peeler. The inside edges of the machine had what appeared to be razor blades, so as the drum whirled round, the blades would peel away the skin and it looked like the drum could change direction to make sure all the skins were removed. There had been no damage reported to the drums or the blades so from an outside appearance no one would have noticed anything wrong. Delores looked closely at the machine, it had thick electrical cables going into a sealed box on the wall next to it, a metal-grate-style lid and a simple green Start, red Stop button on the panel on the outside. Once the potatoes had been peeled there was a hatch on the side of the drum that lifted open, and the now-naked potatoes fell out into the waiting crate below.

'Look at them go!' the inner voice went again. 'It's the potato-based version of the Grand National!'.

"Well now you're being utterly ridiculous," said Agnes to the voice.

At the very bottom of the peeler was a metal door which Delores pulled open. It revealed the mechanics that made the machine work.

"That's way too easy to access," said Agnes. "There must be so many other ways to tamper with this machine if you knew what you were doing, but anyone could open that door and cover the insides with glue."

"This doesn't help narrow down the field of suspects, does it?" said Delores. "It just means that anyone in this entire building could mess with it. And thinking back to what Ellen said, as part of the inductions all new starters get a detailed tour of the factory and they spend a week working down here so everyone feels part of the end product, regardless of what their actual day job is."

"So everyone in this building knows how this machine works," said Agnes. "I'll see if I can get any prints, but I'm not going to hold my breath. The door was the obvious part which would be touched, but let's see if they unknowingly touched anything else down here." Agnes crouched down and took her samples.

They then moved on to part two of the machine, the cutter. Again, they saw it was loaded by hand and was essentially a massive mandolin. Different blades could be inserted to cut different shapes of crisp.

"Ohhhhh, ridges," said Delores, her second most favourite crisp shape.

Once the potatoes had been through the cutter, they were air-blown out of the drum and into another crate waiting for them below.

'And what a transformation challenge that was!' went the inner voice again. 'In goes a plain potato and out comes a crisp of beauty... a crisp cut for one cut crisp!'.

Agnes shook her head quite violently, trying to dislodge the voice.

Delores studied the blades.

"They are sharp," she said. "S.H.A.R.P."

"Please don't cut yourself," said Agnes, "because if you do, all you'll see is the door closing behind me as I exit the building, followed by the screeching of my tyres as I vacate the car park and exit stage left."

"Noted," said Delores, "and the same goes for me, too. Trust me, if you cut yourself, I'm out."

"Glad we're on the same page," said Agnes.

"As long as we're not on the same plaster," replied Delores. "This machine," she said pointing to the cutter, "it's just like the peeler, loaded by hand, simple to operate. And both sets of inner workings are easy to access. Neither machine had the electrics tampered with. The peeler didn't have the... 'peely' bits tampered with..."

"Peely bits'?" said Agnes.

"You know exactly what I mean, and the slicer didn't

have the 'slicey' bits tampered with either. It was just glue, both times. No skill needed; no special parts required – just glue," said Delores.

"So, was it someone from the factory floor who knew to keep the damage simple to spread suspicion, or someone from the offices who kept the damage simple because that's all they could do?" said Agnes.

'Ohhh, what a mystery!' said the inner voice. 'Stay tuned folks to find out who!'.

Agnes glared at her reflection in the drum.

"Shush, shush, shushy shush," she instructed the voice.

"Which means everyone's a suspect," said Delores. "This is unhelpful."

"At this stage, yes," said Agnes. "Okay, so we've come into the factory. We've been washed, peeled and sliced. Where do we go from here?" Agnes followed the floor markings.

"Looks like through another washer. I guess that helps remove any remaining stuck-on peelings and now there's more potato showing, it would clean off another layer of starch. Right, so from washing again we go to..." Delores also followed the floor markings.

"Frying." She looked around. "Surely the slices have to dry out a bit before they get chucked in the vats?"

"Well, for a start," said Agnes, "let's hope they aren't chucked. That would be all sorts of messy. It looks like they air dry after their second washing and then travel along these lines to… yep, look there's another metal bowl. So they end up in that and are then 'placed', Delores, not 'chucked' in the fryer." Agnes looked in the frying cauldron. "Yes, look, there's a basket in it so they must be lifted out when done. It's just a huge deep-fat fryer, but on a massive, massive scale."

'Hot, hot, hot!' went the inner voice. 'Hot, crispy, crunchy slices of deliciousness on their way to being teased and tickled with the seasoning of your choice'. Agnes quietly told the inner voice where it could stick its slices of deliciousness.

"It's one hell of a deep-fat fryer," said Delores.

Agnes looked round for the next part on the potato to crisp transformation.

"Right, so when they're done, they're lifted out and placed... where?"

"Along there," said Delores. They saw that the basket lifted up and could twist around to empty the crisps along another conveyor belt to the drums, where the flavourings could be added whilst the crisps were still warm.

"I was wrong," said Delores.

"About what?" asked Agnes.

"They do have a tumble dryer," she said, pointing to the rotating cylindrical machine.

"Well, quite," said Agnes. "So the crisps go into this machine and go round and round where the flavour seems to be sprayed on."

'Yum yum!' said the depressingly cheerful positive inner voice. Agnes ignored it.

"This was also subject to sabotage, with the flavourings being muddled up." She looked up and saw a tub where the flavourings were added which connected to the sprayer going into the drum. "I wonder where the flavourings are kept?"

They both looked around.

"Over here," said Delores. She walked over to a cage

which was full of sacks labelled with their respective flavours and rattled the door. It was locked.

"Well, that's at least something," said Agnes. "It's probably the most secure area in this entire building. I wonder who's got access?" Delores walked round the cage and found a list of names pinned to the racking on the other side and brought it round to show Agnes.

The list of names was as follows:

Flavouring Manager.

Flavouring Deputy Manager.

Flavouring Shift One Supervisor.

Flavouring Shift One Deputy Supervisor.

Flavouring Shift Two Supervisor.

Flavouring Shift Two Deputy Supervisor.

Factory Manager.

"Oh, hang on," said Agnes, "that's very interesting."

"What's that?" asked Delores.

"It says Factory Manager," said Agnes, pointing to the last job title on the list. "That's Jason Sadler, one of the Secret Santa victims."

"That's not just interesting," said Delores, "that's *very* interesting. That makes it Alice, Charles, Jason and Lizzie, all Secret Santa victims and all who could be implicated by the leaks or sabotage. Makes me feel it's all connected somehow. Whoever did this—"

"…Santa…" interjected Agnes.

"…Rrrright… Santa…" said Delores. "Well, Santa seems to have had quite a vendetta. Clearly these people were on the naughty list and definitely not the nice list."

Agnes photographed the list of names and handed it back to Delores who walked back round the cage and put the list back where she found it. She walked back round to Agnes and said, "Okay, so our lovely crispy crisps are now enrobed with the flavourings so where to now?"

They looked down at the floor markings and followed the line that went away from the sprayer.

"Looks like they move over here next and that would take them to… Quality Control."

The QC line had another whiteboard next to it and a bin marked 'fails'. The whiteboard showed the checks for flavour, appearance, smell and crunch.

"They test for crunch?" said Delores.

"Well, if the oil wasn't hot enough and the potato slices went in still damp they wouldn't crisp up," said Agnes. "Imagine your disappointment if expecting a flavoursome, satisfying crunch and all you get is a moist, limp, soggy crack."

"That is neither a pleasing nor appetising description of my favourite savoury snack," said Delores.

"Which is why that crunch is key," said Agnes. "Right, so we've gone through QC, now where do we go off to next?"

Delores walked along the route the line was leading to. "Looks like packaging next," she said.

This part of the factory looked more automated than what they'd seen so far. The crisps – crunchy not moist – were dropped into the crisp packets which then had a squirt of nitrogen pumped in before being heat sealed.

"Always thought it was just air," said Delores.

Agnes shook her head. "No, nitrogen will keep them fresher for longer whereas oxygen would make them go soft." Agnes took a closer look at the packaging machine.

It looked like each pack of crisps was filled by weight to ensure the same amount were in each pack. The weight could be adjusted depending on the final pack size.

Delores and Agnes again took photos and checked over the inner workings of the machine. It wasn't one that had been tampered with, so they didn't spend overly long here. When they had finished they moved on to the final part of the warehouse. Despatch.

'The end of the line!' said Agnes's inner voice.

"Quite literally," said Agnes.

"What was that?" asked Delores.

"Nothing," said Agnes, "nothing at all."

They found that the despatch area seemed to encompass stock control as well. There were arrows denoting which way to walk and yellow warning lines with forklift truck routes mapped out on them. The racking area wasn't huge, so clearly the turnaround time was quick. No one wanted crisps hanging around gathering dust when they could be out with their customers. Stock control had the same whiteboards as goods in – Monday to Friday, morning and afternoon – but this time for orders expected to leave the factory on lorries, piled high. Or at least to the height of the truck filled with pallet after pallet of crunchy, crispy snacks of joy.

"I'm not sure I believe in that tagline anymore," said Delores, pointing to the wording on the cases of crisps.

"What 'crunchy, crispy snacks of joy'?" asked Agnes.

Delores nodded. "The more I learn, the less joy I feel," said Delores.

"It is a little off-putting," said Agnes, "and definitely, at this moment, more despair than joy."

The stock control area was directly opposite the transport team desks. Yet another whiteboard also marked out Monday to Friday, morning, and afternoon, this one with details of the trucks due to be loaded, including registration, driver and route. All the keys for the trucks were in a glass-fronted locked cabinet. Once more, there was a list of authorised key holders who could access the cabinet to unlock it.

The list of names was as follows:
Transport Manager.
Deputy Transport Manager.
Stock Control Manager.
Stock Control Deputy Manager.
Shift One Manager.
Shift One Deputy Manager.
Shift Two Manager.
Shift Two Deputy Manager.

"And this is where we complete the six," said Agnes.

Delores looked at the list.

"Transport Manager; well, that's Daniel Smythe. Is it a coincidence that the lorry keys go missing and he's on the list as an approved keyholder? He's also a Secret Santa victim. Coincidence or target?"

"That's the question," said Agnes.

"You said this completed the six," said Delores looking round. "Where's the sixth?"

Agnes pointed at the transport board again.

"Look at the name of the driver of Truck Three."

Delores read through the names until she got to… Lee Turner.

"It was Lee's truck that had the tyres slashed and Lee

was a Secret Santa victim. So that's all of them linked to the sabotage and Secret Santa."

"Certainly looks that way," said Agnes.

"Well, block me a hat and call me Harold," said Delores.

"Well I'd rather not but if you insist, Harold," said Agnes, "and anyway, you've seen me block a hat. It didn't go well. In fact, I think you came close to banning me from ever touching any of your millinery materials ever again."

"I agree, it did not go well," said Delores. "Did you think I wouldn't notice that you'd glued the felt to the block?"

"At least I didn't staple this time."

"Small mercy," said Delores. "Do you think we need to look at anything else today?"

"No, I'm happy with what we've done. You?"

"All good. My mind is in overdrive as to what we've seen and learned, and we've still got tomorrow to go, but for now, yeah, I'm all good."

"Okay," said Agnes, "let's leave it at that. When I get back, I'll write up the notes and download the data and photos so we're clear for tomorrow."

"Are you going to mention anything to Ellen when she comes to collect the keys later?" asked Delores.

Agnes shook her head. "No, best not. We've still not seen anything that proves Charlie's guilt or proves his innocence, so in that respect, nothing to tell her. We've found that every event this year seems to be connected and someone definitely has a grudge and they're willing to play the long game. Could it be Charlie? Yes, but have we seen enough to prove that? No. So I'll just say we've conducted a thorough search and it's too early to conclude anything."

"Pretty much the truth then," said Delores.

Agnes nodded her head. "Let's debrief again once I've downloaded all the data and photos, and then go through everything in far more detail. See if there's anything that helps point us in the right direction."

"Sounds good to me," said Delores.

They made their way back to reception and let themselves out before securely locking the doors behind them. Removing the protective clothing they wore in the factory they were struck by two things. One was the cold December air. And the second was the returning waft of cheese and onion.

Eight

Monday, 6th December 2021

Just before 12p.m., Delores and Agnes were joined by Marjory, Esme and Edith at the factory car park.

The bazaar was due to run from 12p.m. to 4p.m. but in two shifts to reduce the number of people in one place. Most of the stalls would be in the car park with some in the canteen, and Delores and Agnes planned to be there all afternoon, with Marjory, Esme and Edith taking the 12p.m.–2p.m. slot before being replaced with Mabel, Doreen, Betty and Lou.

"Morning, both!" called out Marjory.

"Morning, all," said Agnes and Delores in unison.

"Sorry we're a bit late," said Marjory. "We planned to get here a bit earlier, but we had a slight hiccup, so I'm afraid we're one short on the first shift."

"Sorry to hear that," said Delores. "What happened?"

"Edna Crac-Wimple is confined to her room at the home. She's not allowed out."

"Oh no!" said Agnes. "Poor Edna. Is she okay?"

"Oh, she's fine," said Edith, "but she's sulking."

"Why's that?" asked Delores.

"She's finally had her driving licence revoked," said Edith, "and she's *not* happy about it."

"At ninety-two..." said Delores, "surely that's a relief."

"She wasn't in an accident, was she?" asked a concerned Agnes.

Marjory, Esme and Edith shook their heads.

"No," said Esme. "She was arrested for speeding and now she doesn't have a driving licence anymore she's in a stroppy sulk."

"Arrested???" said Delores. "Arrested for speeding??? Oh my!"

"Well, in order of offence," said Edith, "breaking and entering, theft, speeding and then evading arrest." A brief pause ensued.

"Rightttt," said Agnes.

"Okayyyy," said Delores.

"Edna always had a thing for speed," said Marjory. "In her very young youth, she used to race cars under the name of Ed Wimple. Did quite well until she encountered a slimy older man on the circuit who had a predilection for younger males. Well, when he tried it on and found that Ed Wimple was less Ed and more Edna, all hell broke loose."

"I hope he was dealt with by the authorities," said Agnes.

"Oh no," said Esme, "back then it was always considered the woman's fault, regardless of circumstances, so she was banned from all racing circuits for life."

"Ever since then, she's had a healthy disregard for authority," said Edith, "...and speed limits."

"Fair enough," said Delores.

"She managed to break into the Wallway Racetrack last Sunday," said Marjory.

"Stole the keys to a rally Mini," said Esme.

"Did sixty miles an hour up Jellicoe Road," said Edith.

"Took the police on a merry dance all round Yarmouth, and along Caister bypass," said Esme.

Agnes and Delores smiled.

"Got to be honest," said Agnes, "I'm actually impressed."

"Me too," said Delores. "Sixty miles an hour along Jellicoe Road?? That is impressive."

The group of ladies all took a moment to revel in the marvellousness of Edna before moving on to the business of the day.

"You've got the photos of the key people we'd like you to interact with if they turn up," said Agnes.

"Chances are they will," said Delores, "and it doesn't matter how many interactions you have with them. Same goes for Team 2 this afternoon. We need to get a real feel for their behaviours, who they talk to, who they avoid and generally what they get up to."

"The more interactions the better," said Agnes, "so we get consistent feedback across the day."

"Oh, and Ellen hasn't told anyone that we came in yesterday for a look round so let's keep that quiet," said Delores.

The gaggle of ladies nodded in agreement.

"Both Delores and I have stalls here all day, so we'll do a couple of laps, but we'll leave most of the intelligence gathering up to you. I'll keep you supplied with tea, coffee, biscuits and cake to take round and Delores will kit you out with some 'special' headpieces to wear and we'll repeat with Team 2 later. I take it you have your camera phones at the ready to snap away?"

"Right then," said Delores. "Marjory, I've matched your flowery skirt and white blouse to this domed beret style, the peaches and pink tones match your skirt, and the embellishments hide the microphone and transmitter. If anyone asks, it is of course available to hire or buy."

"Presumably without the mic," said Marjory as she crouched down enabling Delores to securely fit it in place.

"You never know," said Delores, "it could open up a whole new sector – I can see it now, the 'MI5 Spooks Range', matches your outfit and weapon of choice. We conceal it so you don't have to."

"Sounds like an excellent business plan to me," said Edith. "You could be on to something!" Delores giggled as she mentally envisaged James Bond-esque spies in a range of hats and headpieces whilst out on missions.

"Just call me 00Milliner," she said. "Okay, for you, Edith, this burgundy wool fedora with a black felt band. The feathers are a mix of both hat colours and I've added a diamanté brooch which will sparkle if the light catches it and also hide the camera flash if it goes off."

"And lovely it looks too," said Edith as she adopted the bowed-head-for-fitting pose. This just left Esme to go.

"For you, Esme, I couldn't decide between a trilby and a pillbox, but in the end I went for the trilby in an emerald green with a saucer-style trim and faux emerald clusters. The space underneath the trilby meant we could get a video-recording camera in but whatever you do, don't agree to anyone else trying on the piece!"

"Looking good, ladies," said Agnes. "With any luck the embellishments, decorations and sparkly bits will get some attention and you'll get some good interactions today and we'll get the footage we need." Agnes turned to Delores. "What have you got for Team 2 this afternoon?"

Delores gestured over to her van and said. "Definitely the pillbox option, and I've matched the colour to the outfit Lou Taylor will be wearing. It's light pink with a band going all the way round of handmade faux flowers in differing shades of pink with white for contrast, the sheer volume of flowers will hide the mic. Then for Mabel Daltrey, a vintage-style cloche in navy with a great big bow on the front hiding mic 2."

"Nice," said Agnes.

"For Doreen Dingall, I'm going for a classic mother-of-the-bride style hat in a sparkling sand colour with bows and feathers and the odd diamanté for good measure and to hide the camera. And finally for Betty Mahoney, I thought I'd go all out with a headband covered in black and white chessboard squares with the surveillance miniatures you gave me, Agnes, in full view, attached on a wire support, but mixed in with other dolls house-style miniatures including mobile phones, a laptop, an old style camera and a camcorder. Everything will light up which should get people taking an interest in it and the working surveillance kit will be disguised in plain sight."

"Sneaky!" said Edith.

"Love it!" said Esme.

"You're quite good at all this hat stuff," said Agnes. "I hope Monsieur Delvene is happy with your work."

"It's hard to tell," said Delores. "As long as I'm not

getting the 'nostril, eyebrow' pincer movement then I'll take it as a win."

As Delores finished attaching Esme's headpiece, Ellen wandered over to say hello. Once greetings had been exchanged, she asked if they'd found anything interesting from yesterday's visit.

"We managed to capture a lot of data and information, but it's going to take a bit of time to go through, Ellen," said Agnes. "I've downloaded everything we went through yesterday and will do the same tomorrow for what we find today. From there we'll be able to fill in some of the blanks and that'll lead us to next steps."

"Today's going to be invaluable though," added Delores. "We'll get so much insight from just talking to everyone and that layered on top of what we've already got, and we'll be well on our way. I promise you, Ellen, as soon as we've figured this one out, we'll let you know."

Ellen gave a faint smile followed by a deep breath.

"I know," she said, "I still can't believe it's come to this, but equally I also know it's the right thing to do."

"One question, Ellen, if I may?" asked Marjory.

"Ask away," replied Ellen.

"What's that smell?"

Ellen took in a deep nasal breath.

"Ahhh, our festive range. Turkey and Bacon crisps rolling off the production line today."

"Lovely," said Marjory, making a mental note to strike turkey from her Christmas Day menu with immediate effect.

The stalls were now fully set up with several local businesses taking part. They were carefully spread out in the car park area to avoid any large groups gathering round with just five further stalls in the factory canteen. Crispin Crisps' staff soon started to come out of the reception doors to take a look round, with the local business owners hoping they could at least make a small profit today to help get them through another Covid-impacted year.

Agnes took up position on her stall. She had run an electrical cable from reception to the stall so she could keep a good supply of tea, coffee and hot chocolate rolling, as well as warm mince pies and sausage rolls. She'd also brought with her a hostess trolley which was now loaded up with goodies, hot drinks' flasks and paper plates and cups. The ladies would go round in rotation selling what they could and when needed, giving away for free if it got the target talking. The staff and attendees from other sites on the industrial estate were able to come out in small regular groups and even those working from home were able to book in a slot to see what was on offer. Agnes could only hope that those on the target list did turn up.

Delores also had her stall set up. Wet weather wasn't forecast but she still erected a gazebo over her stand just in case and then hoped that the wind stayed low. She'd brought in a number of pieces, some new, some old, and had arranged them on her 'head' stands in colour groups. She'd also brought in some of the accessories that she was able to customise on headpieces so she could demonstrate just how well a piece could be personalised to a client's needs. She left in the van the headpieces for Team 2 and a number of back up pieces as well, just in case she did make some sales today. She looked around at the other stalls. There was one selling handmade cards, a candle stand, someone selling jewellery, a stand with lots of knitted items (although from this distance she couldn't tell if one of the items was a tea cosy or a large beanie hat), a handbag stall, a wooden toys and gifts stall and finally a stall selling sweets, jams and potentially, marmalade. This time it was Delores's overly cheerful inner voice that said to her, 'I know what you're thinking'. Delores snorted and said to herself, "Oh, you do, do you?". Her ever cheerful inner voice said 'Yep!'. "Go on then," Delores said back to the voice, grateful there was no one at her stand to hear her talking to herself. 'You're thinking why is marmalade marmalade and not orange jam'. Delores furrowed her eyebrows – her inner voice clearly knew her well. "I might have been thinking that, yes," she said to the inner voice, "but what would you know about these things?". Her overly cheerful voice gave an overly cheerful giggle; Delores wondered if everyone's inner voice was this annoying. 'Well' said her inner voice, 'jams are made using whole fruits like strawberries and raspberries, but marmalade is made using just citrus fruit and then only the peel and juicy bits'. Delores conceded that her inner voice was very well informed. 'I should hope so' said the annoying voice. Delores tried to shush the inner voice and block it out of her mind. It didn't work.

'Delores' the inner voice said.

Delores ignored it.

'Delores' it said again.

Delores ignored it again.

"Delores, you do know it's me, Agnes, talking to you on your earpiece?" asked a still cheerful Agnes.

Delores put her left hand to her left ear and wiggled

a finger. She felt a small object which she had totally forgotten that Agnes gave to her just before the other ladies arrived.

"Yes, absolutely, totally knew it was you," flustered Delores. "Never any doubt."

"Tremendous," said Agnes. "Look over by reception and see who's just come out together."

Delores looked over to see Alice and CC walk out together straight into the path of the roving tea ladies.

Esme and Edith had taken the tea trolley on a slow walk around the car park bazaar. So far none of the people they'd spoken to had been on the watch list, but they were still able to speak to everyone and use their surveillance gear to the max. Over by the candle stand they saw Charles and Ellen, two key targets on the list so they swiftly changed course but mid-way over, they saw Alice and CC come out of the reception doors. With a small change in travelling direction, the tea trolley came to a sudden and abrupt halt in front of reception completely blocking Alice and CC in.

"So sorry about that, my dears!" said Esme.

"This trolley is just so heavy," said Edith, "it's got a mind of its own where it's going."

CC smiled at the poor old ladies trying to steer the trolley.

"Not a problem at all," he said in a loud voice seeing Edith's hearing aid. "You're doing a marvellous job today."

"Although at your age, maybe you should be safely tucked up inside your homes instead of *trying* to help," said a less smiling Alice.

'Aye aye' said Edith's inner voice, 'she's an interesting one. Let's see where we go with this'.

"I'm so sorry," Edith said, looking directly at Alice. "Oh how I long to be your age again. What are you? Fifty? Fifty-five?"

"I most certainly *am not*," said an indignant Alice, putting particular emphasis on 'am' and 'not'.

"Well whatever you are, dear, it's a long way off me," said Edith. "Have you worked here long?"

"Yes," was Alice's brief reply. CC was a bit more friendly.

"This is my family business," he said. "I'm CC, one of the directors, and I've worked here my whole life."

"Imagine that," said Esme. "I bet there's some stories you could tell about this place."

"More than you'd know!" laughed CC.

"And what about you?" said Esme to Alice. "How long have you worked here?"

"Too long," was the blunt reply.

"Well maybe you'll move onto something new sooner than you think," said Edith. "In the meantime, mince pie and tea? We're all gloved up so very hygienic."

"Oh yes please," said CC, trying his best to make up for his surly companion. Edith poured him his hot drink, with his requested milk and one sugar and served one warm mince pie alongside it.

"What about you?" asked Esme to Alice, waving an empty paper cup in her direction.

"No," said Alice.

"Well that's a shame," said Esme, "but we're here all day, so just grab us if you change your mind. We've got tea, coffee, hot chocolate, mince pies and sausage rolls; everything you could possibly want! Now, where did I put my... whoops! Oh silly me!" Esme 'accidentally' dropped the empty paper cup in Alice's direction and Alice, without thinking, put her hand out to catch it. As she handed it back to Esme she sniped, "Mind what you're doing, if that had been full you'd have burnt me."

Esme carefully put the cup on the bottom shelf. She'd write Alice's name on it when they'd moved on. She then looked at Alice to say, "And what a misfortunate event that would have been," with only the slightest hint of sarcasm.

"I've already had one incident here," said Alice, "I don't need another."

"Oh no, my dear, poor you. What happened?" asked Edith, knowing full well what had happened, but wanting to get Alice's take on things.

"Stupid Secret Santa," said Alice. "I only did it to show that managers can take part with the little people as well in these things. Well my stupid gift, from the stupid Secret Santa, was laced with itching powder and my skin has only just recovered so I certainly don't need you pouring hot liquid all over my arms and causing me more grief."

"You poor dear," said Esme. "It sounds like someone's idea of a joke."

"Well it wasn't funny," said Alice before she stormed off.

"Please accept my apologies, ladies," said CC. "She's had a rough time and not in the best frame of mind. But can I just say that your tea and mince pie was lovely."

"You're welcome," said Esme. "Here, let me take your used plate and cup so you don't have to walk round with it." CC handed over the used items, smiled and left them to find Alice. Esme wrote his name on the plate and cup and added Alice's name to the cup she 'caught'.

"I tell you," said Edith, "if I had itching powder, I'd get her as well."

"She is not a nice lady," said Esme. "Do you think they're having an affair?"

"If they are, then I have no idea what he sees in her. He seems to be quite pleasant, but her? No."

"Maybe it's the other way round?"

"How do you mean?"

"Maybe she's using him," said Esme. "After all, with all the strife with Charlie, maybe Alice thinks he'll be cut out and CC will inherit. She strikes me as a power-crazy piece of work, so CC could be her way to the top."

"I'm not sure who'd be worse, her or Charlie," said Edith, looking over to the other end of the car park to see if Charles and Ellen were still around.

"I almost think she'd be worse," said Esme. "She seems full of her own self-importance, and I totally agree, if I had any itching powder on me I'd have sprinkled it all over a mince pie and force fed it to her if necessary."

Up in the canteen, Marjory was also on mince pie duty. There were several stands and small controlled numbers of people were allowed in for a wander. Marjory was in the main wishing she was out on car park reconnaissance because she was sure the smell of turkey and bacon was stronger in here than outside. Glancing round, she could see Charlie at the perfume and aftershave stand so she made a beeline straight towards him.

"Good afternoon," Marjory cheerfully said to Charlie.

"Afternoon," he said back.

"Tea? Coffee? Mince pie?" offered Marjory pointing to her wares.

"As long as it's not crisps – I'll have a tea and mince pie, please," replied Charlie.

"It is a rather pungent smell, isn't it?" said Marjory as she poured his tea.

"Trust me, it wouldn't be that bad if proper ventilation was in place. Things will change when I'm the one in charge."

Marjory wasn't sure if that was a promise or a threat but decided she was going to talk to Charlie for a bit longer, whether he wanted to or not.

Back in the car park, there was a steady, if socially distanced, stream of people going round the stalls. Some were buying, some were just looking. Delores had also sold some of her older ladies' summer stock she'd brought along, and the men's flat caps were going very well. In fact, they were outselling everything else – maybe it was because it was a cold day she thought – and she'd even managed to book in a couple of potential clients for later in January, one for a wedding piece and one for a day at the races. Yes, this was a successful day all round. Delores nipped back to her van to unload another crate of men's caps and when she brought them back to the stall, she saw Anne Mayhew was there. After greetings were over and done with, Anne began to look at the flat caps. Delores, never one to waste a sales and intelligence-gathering opportunity, said to her, "Is it for you or someone else?"

Anne smiled back. "For me please; I don't know anyone to buy something like this for. Aren't they lovely? You're so talented to be able to make something like this. I wouldn't know where to start!"

"Well I do offer classes to anyone who'd like to make

a piece of their own. Hang on two ticks, I've got a leaflet here…" Delores had a rummage under her table and pulled out a stack of leaflets, one of which she gave to Anne.

"A tweed one would suit you, I think this one." Delores reached for a flat cap from the far end of the table and handed it to Anne. "Yes, this one should fit you perfectly." Anne tried it on, and Delores was right, it fitted like a glove.

"How do you do it?" Anne asked. "Seriously, not only can you hand-make the hats, but you can also immediately pick out the perfect one and the perfect fit. I love it… sold!" Delores promptly picked up her payment card machine and within seconds the flat cap was Anne's.

"We're all good at something, Anne, like you as a PA. I wouldn't know where to begin."

Anne smiled, then teared up. "I'm beginning to think I'm not very good at my job, after all," she told Delores.

"Why on earth do you think that?" said Delores. "Look at this amazing event. It wouldn't happen without you."

"It might be amazing now, but what happens when it all goes wrong?" said Anne.

"What makes you think it'll go wrong? This is a brilliantly organised event and you've had to do it with Covid restrictions in place as well. Believe me, not many people could do that."

"It'll go wrong," said Anne, "trust me. I take it you know what happened?"

Delores nodded, before telling a 'not completely' untruth. "Ellen briefly mentioned it had been a bad year for you all when I was booking this event. She was hoping today might cheer everyone up."

Anne continued, "I thought the same about the Secret Santa event but look how that turned out."

"But that wasn't your fault, Anne," said Delores. "You're not to blame for the gifts that people chose to give."

"But if I hadn't pushed it, we'd never have done Secret Santa, but I did and look what happened. It's all my fault. I'm responsible."

"No, you're not."

"Yes, I am. Charles and Ellen were hesitant about doing it this year – we didn't do it last year when Covid was so bad still, but I thought after the horrible year they've had with everything that's been going on, why not run it this year on a smaller scale? I thought it would cheer everyone up a bit – a small slice of festive normality – but look what happened. I wish I'd never pushed them into it and I'm just waiting to find out what's gone wrong today." It was probably a good thing that Anne couldn't overhear the conversation taking place at the very same time on Agnes's stall.

"Sometimes, Anne, these things are out of our control," said Delores, "so just tell yourself that most people got a gift that made them smile and cheered them up a bit, so you did good. Now, have you thought about a matching scarf to go with that hat?"

Agnes was doing well on sales and had several consultations for birthday and Easter cakes, so it looked like Bring on the Cake would have a busy few months in 2022. She took a sip of tea just as a hopefully prospective customer approached.

"Hello there," said Agnes, "can I interest you in anything today?"

The prospective customer looked at what was on offer and then said, "I'm after a fruit cake but I have some special requirements."

"Not a problem," said Agnes, "I can cater for dairy free or gluten free, I just need advance notice to clear down the kitchens to ensure no cross-contamination. What did you have in mind?"

"Oh, I don't want anything like that," said the prospective customer. "I want a fruit cake without any fruit in it."

Agnes frowned a little as she processed the request. "A fruit cake with no fruit in?" she asked, just to check her understanding and to double-check she hadn't zoned out and the customer wanted sugar free.

"A fruit cake without fruit," repeated the customer. Agnes looked round – were there hidden cameras (not installed by her) for this wind-up request?

"So you want a spiced cake?" asked Agnes. "Cinnamon, all spice, nutmeg, cloves… that sort of cake?"

"No, I want a fruit cake, without fruit."

Agnes stared at the customer. "How… in what way… but that's…" Agnes was having to choose her words carefully. "Do you mean no fruit as in no raisins, sultanas or currants? That sort of fruit? Or no apples or pears kind of fruit? Or no lemon or orange citrusy fruit?"

"A traditional fruit cake but without the raisins, sultanas or currants. Can't abide them. They look like little turds."

Agnes remained perturbed. "What about lemon and orange – can they be included?"

"That would be acceptable."

"Right, and the spice mix… cinnamon, all spice, nutmeg, cloves?"

"Acceptable."

"So it's a spice cake," said Agnes.

"No, I want a fruit cake without the fruit, not a spice cake." Agnes looked round half expecting a demented TV host with camera to pop out of a bush and shout 'Surprise!!'. Agnes looked back at the customer.

"I can make you a cake with flour, eggs, butter, dark sugar, black treacle, spices, lemon and orange zest but no fruit. Would that be acceptable?"

"Yes, that's a fruit cake without the fruit. I'll want it to feed ten and need it for the end of January."

"I tell you what," said Agnes, "here's my card. Why don't you come in and see me and we can make your order official? I'll cost it up ahead of time, so you know what you're looking at."

"Well, I hope I'll be looking at a fruit cake with no fruit but give me your card and I'll phone you to arrange my visit." With this, the mysterious customer huffed off to the next stall to demand earrings but not for pierced ears. Agnes heard the stallholder mention 'clip-ons' before the customer angrily replied back that they didn't want 'clip ons'; they wanted earrings not for pierced ears. Agnes simply wrote in her diary, 'spiced cake… potential weirdo'. She paused and then crossed out the word 'potential'.

Nine

Thursday, 9th December 2021

The following Thursday, Agnes and Delores plus Marjory, Esme and Edith met up in the agency office for a full debrief. Once hot drinks and nibbles had been offered and consumed, they sat around the conference table to review Monday's findings. Marjory had collated Team 2's feedback as well so there was much to go through.

"Right then," said Agnes, "thoughts on what you saw. Were you able to catch all the Secret Santa victims and did anyone else come across the very strange individual with very strange purchasing requirements?"

"We saw both," said Marjory. "The extremely strange individual that no one seemed to know who they were or why there were there, and yes, we saw all the Secret Santa victims across the day – they all attended at varying times. Team 1 got three out of six Secret Santa victims and those who didn't take up the hot drink or nibble had the full 'tea and biscuits' experience. Team 2 got the stranger as well, just in case there is some outside force in play as their appearance seemed all too strange. They also tracked down the required Secret Santa victims 4, 5 and 6, plus some repeat interactions with victims 1 to 3. Across both teams we got a whole host of others as well so between us we got them all."

"Lovely," said Delores.

"I've not had a chance to review the footage, photos or run the prints yet," said Agnes. "That's my next job. Who knew at this time of year that a bakery selling festive Christmas food would be so popular! Mince pie, anyone?"

"As long as it's not a Turkey and Bacon crisp then yes please," said Marjory. "Seriously did you get the whiff as well on Monday? The concentrated odour was not a pleasant olfactory experience." As everyone nodded, Edith took up the debrief.

"Our first target was Alice Alderman." Esme scowled at the mere mention of Edith saying her name. Edith continued. "Quite frankly a nasty piece of work. Rude, spiteful and full of her own self-importance."

"She was like it with both us and Team 2," said Esme, "and when we watched her with other more junior members of staff, she was just the same. In fact, the only people she was vaguely human to were the directors."

"How about her and CC?" asked Delores, thinking back to when they found the diary in Alice's desk with CC's initials in it.

"She definitely behaved better with him, but even he had to smooth things over now and again," said Esme.

"Quite frankly, Delores," said Edith, "whoever gave her the itching powder-laced toiletries should be knighted or made a dame for services for paying back a bully."

"To get to where she is now, she's either very good at her job and very good at smooth-talking management into ignoring any concerns her team has about her, or she's rubbish at her job, relies on her team to do the work and make her look good, whilst she's smooth-talking management and talking them into ignoring any concerns they have about her," said Esme.

"So what I'm hearing then, is that Alice isn't actually a very nice person, and her Secret Santa gift was very deliberately targeted at her. She's clearly wound someone up so much, they've maybe snapped and they saw their chance to get back at her," said Delores. Marjory, Esme and Edith nodded their heads very enthusiastically.

"How about CC?" asked Agnes.

"He does seem very nice," said Marjory. "He was very personable and cheerful to all at the event, including us, and ensured he went round speaking to everyone several times."

"He was the same with Team 2," said Esme. "They watched him closely after their 'Alice' run-in to see what he'd do, but he genuinely came across as a nice, fairly gentle, relaxed laid-back soul."

"He didn't seem at all put out that Charles had inherited the business and not him. I think that although he's a director of the family firm and by all accounts good at his job, he has a sense of relief and lightness that ultimately the success of the business is firmly on Charles's shoulders and not his," finished Edith.

"Talk to us about Charles and Ellen," said Agnes. "They were there all afternoon and put in several appearances that I saw."

Marjory paused for a moment to gather her thoughts before speaking.

"Charles… now he gives a very good show at going round to talk to everyone – like CC did – but with Charles, I felt it was more forced than natural. Not that he didn't want to do it, but you could tell it wasn't something that came easily to him."

"I agree," said Edith. "Nice enough chap but you can see a figurative weight being lifted from him when he's back in his 'safe' family group or when he's on his way back to his office."

"He says he's a 'people person' and I think he genuinely believes he's got his staff's best interests at heart in everything he does, but that maybe doesn't come across to the staff that way," said Esme. "Some of the staff we chatted to definitely didn't like the fact that he and the other directors were all sitting in one 'exclusive' part of the office and not at the beating heart of the business."

"Enough to make someone target him in Secret Santa?" asked Agnes. The ladies looked thoughtful.

"Potentially," said Marjory, "but just because he finds it difficult in large groups of people and likes to hide away in his office doesn't seem like a very good reason for someone to gift him that jigsaw."

"Although, compared to what the others had, where their gifts caused an unpleasant physical reaction," said Edith, "Charles just had a jigsaw, with a meaningless phrase on it. So his gift could have been from a disgruntled employee but unlike the others, not one who wanted to cause him actual harm."

"Good point," said Delores. "What about Ellen?"

"She's a peacemaker. Tries to smooth things over between Charles, Charlie and Lizzie. Then tries to be the more human link between Charles and the rest of the staff. She's obviously got a huge job anyway being Finance Director so is under massive pressure from that, and then on top of that as a family business, trying to keep the family on one side," said Marjory.

"The staff like her," said Esme. "No one had a bad word to say about her. She's kind and generous, she's approachable, willing to listen and helps out where she can. Even when the factory was struggling in the first lockdown having so many off with Covid, she rolled up her sleeves and pitched in on the production line."

"Which means she had a very good working knowledge of not just how the production machines work but everything that's entailed getting the orders out of the door. And that includes the trucks and transport processes," countered Edith.

"You don't think she's linked to the sabotage?" asked an incredulous Delores.

"My Security Services training wouldn't rule anyone out," said Edith. "She obviously had access to all the company finances, full access to the factory and she was in Secret Santa but didn't get a bad gift. She'd know that it would be very easy to pin the blame on Charlie as well. So no, I wouldn't rule her out until the evidence says otherwise." Delores conceded that Edith was right in her thinking, but seriously, how could anyone suspect Ellen?

"What were your thoughts on Charlie?" asked Agnes, keen to move the conversation on.

"Charlie probably surprised us the most," said Marjory.

"Really... how?" asked Agnes.

"He appeared when we were there, but Team 2 didn't see him. I have to be honest and say that he came across very well. He wasn't at all what we'd been led to believe."

"Charlie?" asked Delores. "Are you sure it was him, Charlie?"

"Definitely him," said Marjory. "He was actually more like Ellen and CC. He spoke to everyone, he was nice, he was relaxed... almost jolly."

"Jolly as in Santa jolly?" asked Agnes. "Secret Santa jolly?"

"Yes and no," said Marjory, somewhat confusingly.

Edith stepped in. "Potentially but he could be a Jekyll and Hyde character," she explained. "He got on well with the staff, well with the stallholders – he must have come round to you both?" she said to Agnes and Delores.

"Well, yes he did, and I have to admit he was quite nice," said Agnes, "but I wondered if that was more an act than reality."

"Same here," said Delores.

"No, I really think he was being genuine," said Edith.

"But that doesn't tie in with what Ellen's said about him," said Delores.

"And that's your Jekyll and Hyde character," said Edith. "As Jekyll, he's a nice bloke to the staff and they get on well with him. Even some of his improvement ideas make sense, like better security in and around the site and automating some of the machinery so they don't need human intervention and therefore can't be messed with." Delores sighed – she was reminded of her conversation with Andrew in the car park when her and Agnes surveyed the factory.

"Actually, that does tie in with what I was told when we did our factory visit on Sunday. The group I was talking to said what a good bloke Charlie was and how he'd helped one of them out when his car broke down. He also donated a fair chunk of money to their charity day as well."

"That's so not the Charlie that Ellen talks about though," said Agnes.

"And that's where Hyde comes in," said Edith. "When it comes to family, Charlie is a whole different person. We saw his body almost tense up with anger when a family member was nearby. If he spoke to Ellen, Charles or Lizzie he was surly and he became a hormonal teenager again full of rage and angst."

"He also genuinely thinks his ideas are what's best to secure the future of Crispin Crisps," said Marjory. "Fewer staff, more machines, more products, more sales, more profit. In his view, everything needed to keep Crispin Crisps going for the next generation. He's angry that Charles hasn't retired yet (as his father did before him) and handed the factory keys over to the next generation. It doesn't look like Charles is going anywhere soon so all Charlie can see is his destiny getting further and further away and with it his chance to make his changes."

"What does the next generation look like though – after Charlie?" asked Agnes.

"He's divorced but has two kids," said Esme, "a boy called Christopher and a girl called Carly. They're both early twenties now; I think Chris is in his final year at university and Carly is on a gap year. Christopher will eventually inherit the factory after Charlie, but, because Charlie sees his time at the top being still so far away and even then, when he gets there, his time being limited, he's kind of taken it out on Christopher so they don't get on that well."

"Jekyll and Hyde," said Edith.

"He skipped the family tradition then of calling the oldest son Charles," said Agnes.

"That comes back to Jekyll and Hyde again," said Esme. "At face value, to annoy his family, no, he didn't call the boy Charles. But where Charlie has the absolute belief that his future of the factory is in his hands, he used Charles as the boy's second name."

"Oh, so Christopher Charles Crispin," said Agnes. "... another CC... no, a CCC!"

"It does mean though that Charlie had a lot to gain by sabotaging the factory machinery," said Delores. "He's proving his point how easily the whole operation can be brought down by lack of progress, and if he's got that much of a downer on his family, the best way to get back at CC would be to target Alice in Secret Santa – even if she is a cow and we'd all vote for her to eat the unmentionable parts of a scorpion in a TV phone-in competition line. He'd also know that Lizzie as Supply Chain Director would be both personally and professionally embarrassed when the supplier invoices and wholesale orders were negatively impacted and don't forget both his sister and father were Secret Santa victims, so he's had opportunity to get all of them."

"You said you found the list on Anne Mayhew's desk of all the Secret Santa players?" asked Edith. Agnes nodded her head.

"That's also on my list to go through as well, as we'll need to engineer some offline conversations with everyone to see if they'll come clean about the name they pulled out of the Santa hat. There were only eighteen players, and we already know who six were, so hopefully the other twelve will be easy to track down and speak to."

"What about Ellen though?" asked Esme.

"The false financial information at the start of the year," said Delores, "the bank loan, the tax affairs, all false information which not only made the company look bad but also his mother as well as Financial Director. All along he's had the means, the motive and the opportunity to cause trouble."

"He has," said Edith, "but again, until you've got the evidence to prove it, you've got nothing."

"It's all quite mind-boggling," said Agnes. "Let's move onto Lizzie. How did you find her?"

"Lizzie wasn't there to start with," said Marjory, "but she appeared when Team 2 were in place. Their feedback on her was very interesting."

"In what way?" asked Agnes. Marjory referred to Team 2's notes.

"She's got elements of Charles, Ellen and Charlie about her. She did her walk round of the stalls and was polite and pleasant but in a muted way."

"That sounds about right," said Delores. "When she came to my stall, she said the right words but there wasn't any warmth there, but equally nothing nasty either."

"She'll talk to people but keep her guard up, and she'll help someone if she likes them but won't if she doesn't. Like Charlie, she has a problem with her family, although for different reasons, but unlike Charlie who seems to get on with all the staff, Lizzie only gets on with her chosen few," said Marjory.

"What's her problem within the family?" asked Agnes.

"She has major beef with Charlie," said Esme. "*She* genuinely believes his lack of ideas and vision for the future are bad and thinks he's bullying her when he won't listen or take on board any suggestions she has. She's jealous that he'll inherit the company even though she's the oldest."

"It does seem unfair in this day and age that the oldest son inherits the business, just because he's the oldest son," said Delores.

"I agree," said Esme, "but when the company was founded in 1950 by the first Charles Crispin, it was just the way the world was back then. The oldest son inherits the business, and he enshrined it in a legal covenant covering the business. No one's ever changed it or challenged it in a court of law, which I imagine would be very expensive in lawyers' fees alone."

"Lizzie feels she doesn't get taken seriously by her parents," continued Edith. "Team 2 heard various snippets of information, particularly in the ladies' loos where conversations over cubicles flowed freely. Charles refuses point blank to discuss the inheritance with her; as far as he's concerned the factory will always go to the oldest son and he's told Lizzie if she ever challenged it, she's out. She earns a decent wage but doesn't have any private income behind her to challenge anything legally so unless Charles made the decision and updated the covenant, the factory is Charlie's, even if Charles does fear for the future under him."

"But all this means though," said Agnes, "is that Lizzie could equally be the year-long saboteur and for the same reasons as Charlie. She had access to the emails, the machinery and the transport yard to cause a million pieces of chaos, knowing that Charlie would ultimately get the blame as his resentment to his family was far more vocal and brutal than hers."

"What about Secret Santa though?" said Delores. "She was also a victim, unless she sent herself her own gift."

"That is the one sticking point," said Agnes, "but maybe she also wound up someone who isn't in her chosen group, and they decided to have their revenge." Delores looked at the ladies.

"So far it seems that Charles and CC seem unlikely as the perpetrators," – there were nods around the table – "but Ellen… and I do find that very difficult to believe… and Charlie and Lizzie are up there as key suspects."

"Yes," said Marjory, Esme and Edith all together.

"Well, we're about as far away from 'crunchy, crispy snacks of joy', as we could possibly get," said Agnes.

"It still leaves us with Daniel, Lee and Jason," said Delores, "although at this rate, maybe we should also just move them straight from the Victim board to the Suspect board."

"Go on then," said Agnes, "what've you got on this lot?" Once more Marjory consulted her notes.

"These three were on Team 2's radar, none of them went to any stalls outside, just the ones in the canteen, and based on Team 2's feedback you should be looking to group this lot as one single 'being' instead of three individuals."

"Why's that?" asked Agnes.

"Apparently, and you'll see from the photos, Daniel, Lee and Jason came in the canteen with about six other blokes. All were wearing black safety boots (as you'd expect), but then matching dark indigo-style jeans, plain long-sleeved white or blue shirts – sleeves rolled up to the elbow – and still in hi-vis jackets. They moved as one group instead of going off in different directions. When they left the factory at 4p.m. after their shift ended, they were even all wearing the same suit-style jacket with reinforced elbow patches. They went round each stall in the canteen but only in their 'gang', none of them bought anything and then they all sat together having their lunch. Team 2 said they were a bit loud and 'laddish' in behaviour but seemed to get on well as a contained group and well with anyone else they came into contact with if they were also 'laddish.'"

"What about anyone who didn't fall into that group?" asked Delores.

"Pretty much ignored them," said Marjory. "Team 2's view was that whoever each of their respective Secret Santa gifters were, it could just have been 'one of the lads' taking the gift a bit too far."

"Like a sense of humour failure?" asked Delores.

"Possibly," said Marjory. "It's like their behaviour within their group can be a bit rough and ready and they know how far to push each other within their group boundaries but did their gifters read the room wrongly and take their joke presents too far?"

"It's an interesting thought," said Agnes. "It sounds like their mindset at work is purely limited to their immediate group and they're switched off from the wider business.

Team 2 raise a good point about their Secret Santa gifters coming from that same small mindset."

"What about the non-family directors?" asked Delores. "I didn't see any of them all afternoon so assumed they just stayed inside?"

"Malcolm Carson had a long weekend so wasn't in work on the Friday before the bazaar or the Monday," said Marjory, "so we didn't get anything on him yet, but if needed, we know where he lives so can do the necessary if required."

"Jayne Johns was there," said Esme. "She stayed inside and didn't really mix much with anyone else apart from her legal secretary and Anne Mayhew. She was polite enough but gave off an aura of 'I'm a director and I don't really want to spend that much time with the little people'. Team 2 described her as cold."

"And Richard Coates, HR Director?" asked Delores.

"He's a funny one," said Esme.

"Funny ha ha, or funny odd?" asked Agnes.

"Odd," replied Esme, Edith and Marjory as one.

"He is unremarkably remarkable," said Marjory. "Unremarkable in that you'd pass him in the street and not notice he was there, yet remarkable as to how someone like him could have become a director and an HR director at that."

"I watched him talk to some of the staff," said Esme. "Afterwards, I *accidentally* bumped into them with the trolley and got talking about him – they had no idea who he was – they thought he was either a stallholder or just some random person off the street who'd turned up to look round the stalls for some shopping."

"There were times when I thought even he didn't know who he was or what day of the week it was," said Marjory.

"Is he unwell or just incompetent?" asked Agnes.

"I'd say incompetent," said Marjory. "He must have been able to talk the talk to get as far as he has in life, but he comes across as totally inept and only one foot in reality. God only knows what he does if someone goes to him with an HR query." Marjory shuddered at the thought.

"You said you took a copy of the list from Anne Mayhew's desk of all the Secret Santa players?" asked Edith. Agnes nodded and reached out behind her to grab a copy for them to review the names.

"These three," she said pointing to the names, "are regulars at the bakery so I can get them talking to see who they ended up with and what they bought."

"And this one," said Delores, "is coming to see me for a headpiece for a christening so I can work on her, so that leaves eight to check."

"Leave it with us," said Marjory. "We'll track them down and get what you need. We'll report back once done."

"Thank you, ladies," said Delores. "We'd be lost without you. As ever you've got us a ton of intelligence and we've got a load of work to do now to go through it all and try and make sense of what's been happening and quite literally whodunnit. We'll await your update with those final name checks." With this the ladies took their leave (along with more mince pies) leaving Agnes and Delores to digest everything they'd found.

"Which job do you want to take on first?" Agnes asked Delores.

"I'll take photos and video footage," said Delores. "You can have fingerprints and all the electrical downloads."

"Sounds like a plan," said Agnes.

Ten

Friday, 10th December 2021

On the morning of 10th December, Agnes and Delores were both in their respective places of work, juggling their day jobs and the Crispin Crisps case. Delores was sat at her workbench thinking 'happy hat thoughts' when her mobile started to ring.

Jumping out of her skin, she reached over to pick it up but missed and instead managed to stick her hand in the box of blocking pins acupuncturing herself six times. Thinking unladylike thoughts and breathing through the pain, she reached over again to pick up her phone; this time, promptly dropping it as drips of blood started to leak from her punctured finger. She bent down to pick up the phone from the floor and in one swift, deft move, banged her head on the workbench. The unladylike thoughts upgraded themselves to very vocal, unladylike words which could only be described as **bold**, *italic*, and <u>underlined</u>. The mobile continued to ring as if taunting her, the ringtone increasing in volume. It also seemed to Delores that it was ever demanding in tone, demanding to be answered straight away. In the position of head under bench, Delores grabbed the phone and answered it.

"Hi, Sarah, sorry for the delay in answering," she said somewhat breathlessly.

"No problem, Delores. Sorry to disturb. Is it a bad time?" the voice now known as Sarah said.

"No, not at all," said Delores. "I was actually just thinking that this shade of blood is exactly the red I need for a piece I'm working on." Sarah knew Delores well enough not to ask more questions.

"Anyway," Delores continued, "how can I help?"

"Well, actually, I think it's the other way round," said Sarah.

"Oh really, how's that?" asked Delores.

"Well," said Sarah, "Marjory sent an alert via secure channels to all groups about your Crispin Crisps case and I think I have something you'll be interested in."

"I'll take any information going," said Delores. "Two ticks whilst I get a pen."

Delores made her way up from under the workbench until she was sat back on her chair again. And if anyone else was looking at her workbench, they would have had no idea where to find a pen. But Delores and her Delorganised way of working knew that a stack of pens was under the latest copy of the *Millinery Masters* magazine, which in itself was under the sinamay, next to the hot glue gun to the left. She deftly picked up a pen whilst at the same time dripping a few drops of blood onto a white plate, which was also on her desk, but ensuring she didn't drop them on her breakfast flapjack which was also on said plate. A blood-flavoured flapjack was as appealing to her as a

Cajun Squirrel crisp. She could colour-match the blood after the call had ended now she had captured her sample, she thought to herself.

"Pen's ready," she said to Sarah. "Go ahead." And Sarah began.

"Marjory sent out the case summary to all our members including the timeline of events, the key players and… well… one bit just doesn't add up."

"Okay," said Delores, "which bit in particular?"

"Do you remember me telling you about the trip me and Eric took?"

Delores nodded her head even though Sarah couldn't see the nod. "I do yes, you mentioned it in one of our Zoom calls back in October. How was it?"

"Oh my, totally amazing. Absolutely stunning. Trip of an absolute lifetime. But I actually think you'll be more interested in what happened on the way back."

"I'm not quite sure what could be better than your trip, but I'm all ears to find out… actually, hang on a moment, let me put my headphones in, then I'll definitely be all ears."

"Sure," said Sarah.

Delores's hand went straight to her headphones which were under a top hat she had just finished blocking and she quickly plugged them in.

"Ready when you are, Sarah," she said. With pen at hand and notepad open for notes, she began to jot down what Sarah was telling her. Every now and again Delores could be heard going… "Uh-huh"… followed by… "Really?"… "Are you 100% certain?"… "And that was definitely who you saw?"… "And that was definitely the date?"… "Really?"…

"Oh, if you've got photos that would be magic"... "Yeah, totally"... "Send me the photos, all the details"... "Completely agree, absolutely unexpected and not what we've been told"... "Well, I look forward to hearing about the trip another time"... "Uh-huh"... "You were right, this is definitely interesting, very interesting"... "Okay, take care".

Delores ended her call with Sarah and for a moment or two, just sat there staring at her notes. She frowned as she mentally went over the case and what this new information meant, thinking back to just a couple of weeks ago when Ellen was sitting in this very workshop, telling her and Agnes everything that had happened. Delores pursed her lips together and then whispered to herself, "Why did she lie?"

*

Agnes, at this same moment in time, was just taking out of the oven another batch of mince pies. Even though she'd made hundreds... no... thousands in her time, the smell was always Christmas to her. In fact, quite often Agnes thought the smell of Christmas, the tree, the tinsel, the cake, the Christmas pudding and the mince pies was better than actual Christmas itself. She started to wonder if she could come up with an Essence of Christmas and use it in her bakes. Surely it wouldn't be too hard to use some perfumery skills with safe-to-eat food ingredients to create that perfect festive aroma? Agnes could see it now: a customer would open a box of mince pies or lift the lid off a Christmas cake box and get that whole smell of Christmas at the same time. An olfactory Christmas gift, she thought to herself, making a mental note to add this to her 2022 To-do List.

With the last batch of mince pies out of the oven, Agnes sat at the table and opened her laptop. She went back over the Crispin Crisps case… the events that took place… the dates they happened, and the people involved. She just had to finish going through the fingerprints they'd amassed and that would then be everything logged from the searches and surveillance. Glancing at her To-do List for today, she crossed off mince pies and upon seeing she had some calls to make picked up her mobile phone. She went into the contacts list and scrolled through to find a name before dialling it. The phone on the other end only rang a few times before a voice answered.

"Agnes… hello! Long time no speak!" said a cheery voice.

"Hello, Mike," she said. "How are you doing?"

"Can't complain, can't complain," said the voice now known to be Mike. "Well actually, I do complain, and I complain quite regularly, but besides from that what can I do for you?"

"I need your help please, on a case we're working on."

"Sounds exciting," said Mike. "What do you need and what's in it for me?"

"Free bread and cakes are what you get. And no, you don't get the what or the why due to client confidentiality, you know that!"

"Shame," said Mike, "but what do you need? If it's in my gift to give, it's yours to receive."

"I was wondering if I could come in and have a look at your servers," said Agnes.

"Looking for anything in particular?" asked Mike, ever the enquiring contact.

"Just some data that you've got. Need to see if I can trace something, but I want to see the source."

"OK," said Mike, "but are you sure it wouldn't be quicker for you just to hack our systems and find what you need anyway?"

Agnes laughed. "I deny everything," she said, "and anyway, don't you want the free cakes?"

"As you know, I will take cake any day of the week, and if it's free cake, all the better. When do you want to pop in?" asked Mike.

"Monday, 10a.m. if that's good for you?"

"Sure," said Mike, adding "see you then. But don't forget the cake," before he rang off.

Agnes knew full well she had already hacked the server and got what she needed; she just hadn't had a chance to look through it yet. But there were just some contacts she had that she knew she had to keep on her side and let them think they knew best. Especially for those cases when they needed to suppress something getting out into the wider world. Or at least, until it was out of their hands and the stories were written regardless. Anyway, she needed to ask Mike something about Armadillo and that definitely couldn't be done via hacking.

Agnes was pleased. That was another task ticked off from her list this morning. She was on a roll. Opening her laptop next, she had four emails in her inbox from a council contact. Each email had a link to another site which opened up some video footage. The videos were of a specific location, on some specific days Agnes had asked for. She fast-forwarded through most of the footage until something caught her eye. She frowned and reversed the video back to play it again. She frowned again, and once more rewound and replayed the footage. Frowning further she zoomed in as best as she could on the freeze-framed picture. The footage got a bit grainy, but she could definitely make out a person, in a place they weren't meant to be, on a day they weren't meant to be there. Agnes picked up her mobile and dialled another number.

"Well, hello stranger. How are you?" said a voice.

"Morning, Julian," said Agnes. "I'm good, how about you?"

"Not too bad," said the voice now known to be Julian, "not too bad at all. Anyways, what can I do you for?"

"I was wondering if you could spare me an hour tomorrow?" asked Agnes.

"Let me check," said Julian, "I don't think I've got anything on but hang on two seconds."

There was a pause until he came back on the line.

"Yep, I can do tomorrow morning, but I need to be back home by 12p.m."

"That's perfect," said Agnes, "thank you. Can you do 8a.m.? I'll text you the address."

"That'll be fine," said Julian. "Is the full kit required?"

"Yes, please," said Agnes. "It won't take long, but it will be a huge help on this case."

"Happy to help," said Julian, "see you tomorrow and if you've got any spare cupcakes going bring those as well."

"Fab, thank you," said Agnes, ending the call and sending the text with the address on.

Julian texted back straight away with 'Got it. See you tomorrow'.

Agnes put her phone back on her desk and smiled to herself. It never ceased to amaze her how many contacts were happy to give information as long as they got free cake. She looked at the footage on her laptop screen and played it back one more time.

"Well, well, well," she said out loud.

Eleven

Monday, 20th December 2021

It had been a busy few days for Agnes in the bakery, so she had only just caught up with what she'd found out with Mike and Julian's help a couple of days ago before she was able to overlay this with what they knew so far. Agnes mulled things over as she made her way to the agency office – Delores was already there updating the case with what she'd found as well and between them, they'd map everything to the timelines already noted and cross-reference with the amassed evidence.

Agnes parked her car next to Delores's, however she opted to park in front of the hedge and not in it, then made her way into the office. Upon entering she opened her mouth to call out 'hello' to Delores but stopped in her tracks when she saw Delores stood bolt upright, her back towards Agnes and her arms outstretched at a taut 90 degrees, frozen to the spot barely breathing. Agnes's internal security dial moved from DEFCOM 5 (Normal) to DEFCOM 4 (Alert). Agnes mentally replayed in her mind the day's events; none of the alarms or alerts she'd installed had gone off, the anti-virus, anti-hacking software was working as normal, so it had to be something else. Agnes's internal security dial moved from DEFCOM 4 to DEFCOM 3 (Prepare). Delores remained unmoved and barely breathing. Agnes ruled out an intruder and even though Armadillo was good, she knew their defences were better so it must be something else. Internal security dial moved from DEFCOM 3 to DEFCOM 2 (Ready to Deploy). Agnes felt a surge of panic go through her... was it a spider... a really big spider... a really big, massive *spider*... a really big massive *spider* with twelve legs and sixteen eyes kind of *spider*! Agnes looked round but she couldn't see anything resembling a ninety-five-legged hairy beast the size of a giant horse, planning to attack and eat them – after all, what other kind of spider was there? Agnes considered then dismissed this thought (except not entirely dismissed, because a ninety-five legged spider is completely untrustworthy and will lull you into a false sense of security until *bam*! Too late – it ate you). Delores remained as still as a marble statue. Agnes's internal security dial moved from DEFCOM 2 to DEFCOM 1 (Immediate Response Maximum Force). Wasp! Wasp! *It must be a stripey little git wasp*, thought Agnes, even in December those little gits were out to get you. Wasp! Wasp! Agnes listened carefully. She could neither hear nor see anything resembling a wasp and come to think of it, Delores was such an animal person, she'd try to capture a ninety-five-legged hairy spider, or a stripy little git wasp and release them back into the wild, whereas Agnes would run away screaming then dial the Army, Navy, Coastguard and Royal Air Force to deploy heavy artillery and dispose of said threat in the quickest way possible. With a slow and steady breath, Agnes's internal security dial moved back from DEFCOM 1 (Immediate Response Maximum Force) to DEFCOM 3 (Prepare).

"Delores?" said Agnes. Delores didn't move.

"Delores!" said Agnes again. Slowly, very slowly, Delores, keeping her arms at a taut 90 degrees, turned to face Agnes. Her pirouette complete, Agnes saw that Delores's face was as red as a beetroot and contorted in pain. Internal security dial moved back up from DEFCOM 3 (Prepare) to DEFCOM 2 (Ready to Deploy).

"Can you tell me what's happened?" asked Agnes. Delores just about managed to shake her head.

"Can you try?" asked Agnes. With her arms still outstretched,

Delores pointed to her handbag. Agnes looked at the bag – it seemed pretty normal to her.

"I'm going to need a bit more to go on; can you try again?" she said. Delores scrunched up her face and managed to let out a growly whisper. "Mixed up my roll-on deodorant and roll-on extreme heat muscle relaxant," she managed to utter. "I'm on *fire… fire… fire…*" Agnes clamped her lips together as tight as she could to stop a snort of laughter exiting her mouth.

"*Fire!*" uttered Delores again. Agnes could hold it no longer; a snort of laughter came forth, long and loud.

"Would you like me to waft your pits with a fan?" Agnes managed to say in between the tears of laughter.

"Step away…" whispered Delores, "step away from the pits." It took several minutes before Agnes could stop laughing, which for Delores felt like several years, before the burning hot sensation subsided enough for her to bring her arms down and sit back at her desk.

"Are you feeling better now?" asked Agnes.

"My hot glue gun doesn't hurt that much," said Delores shuddering, "but I can confirm with total and utter confidence that the use of the word 'intense' to describe the level of heat as written on that roller, is one hundred percent accurate."

"I'd offer you some ginger cookies," said Agnes, "but there's so much ginger powder and stem ginger in them I think you'd ignite again."

"The day I say no to a ginger cookie is the day you know I've been swapped out for an interloper. Three, please."

With tea in one hand and a ginger cookie in the other, Agnes and Delores stood in front of the whiteboards once more.

"Let's take them one at a time in date order," said Delores. "The emails in January and February." Agnes looked at another whiteboard which summarised the evidence they had gathered over the course of their investigation and the photo of Santa, their chief suspect.

"The evidence is watertight on this one," she said. "We've got digital footprints both at sender and receiver level to prove it and it also explains…" Agnes pointed to a place on the whiteboard.

Delores nodded in agreement. "Which takes us to HMRC. Santa upped their game and tried to cause more serious problems when the email campaign failed."

"The problem for Santa is that anything done digitally now, and that's pretty much anything… can be traced.

They might not be breadcrumbs anymore, but the digital dots only lead to one place," said Agnes.

"No doubt, is there?" said Delores. Agnes shook her head. "Okay, so Santa changes tack again and goes for a physical bout of sabotage."

"Which is a bold move," said Agnes. "This time Santa had to be there in person so a far bigger risk this time of being seen."

"Although," said Delores, "we never see Santa deliver the gifts on Christmas Eve, so it's very in keeping with the season." Agnes stared at Delores.

"Did you not take your medication today?" she said. Delores ignored her.

"Three months of sabotage, which at any other time could be considered unlucky single incidents—"

"—But in between what came before and after..." interjected Agnes.

"...Is a very unlucky sandwich," said Delores, "but with a side order of supplier sabotage, so back to digital again." Agnes looked at the evidence board.

"It also goes to show that even if you think you're on your own, flying under the radar..."

"Just like Santa and his sleigh," said Delores.

"...You'll still leave a trail. Unintentional, but almost impossible not to."

"So then we come to Secret Santa," said Delores, "although I think you're right. Satan Santa seems far more accurate. Do you think this was the pinnacle of events or would it have got worse?"

"I think it would have become far worse," said Agnes. "The events at the start of the year were embarrassing or inconvenient which is why the police didn't take it seriously, but the Secret Santa 'gifts' were deliberate against these six people. If it was just this as a standalone event, again you could say they were simply bad jokes but put it with everything else and it becomes a much bigger threat."

They both checked the evidence board one final time. There was absolutely no doubt in their minds, the evidence had been checked, double-checked, and verified thrice more.

"So now all we need to do is present this back to Ellen," said Agnes.

"I am not looking forward to doing that," said Delores. "When do you think we should tell her?"

"Well, for a start I think we need everyone there, including the Secret Santa victims, but I don't think we should do it before Christmas. The factory's shut anyway for the festive break so maybe just after?"

"Let me text Ellen," said Delores. "We'll need her to rally the troops and make sure they all attend so I guess the actual date is on her." Delores picked up her mobile from her desk, shuddering as she saw the roll-on deodorant and roll-on extreme heat muscle relaxant still lying next to one another in her bag. She felt herself getting all hot and bothered again. Why, oh why, did she have to pick today for wearing man-made fibres. She quickly sent the text and whilst waiting for Ellen to reply, asked Agnes, "How are things looking with Armadillo?"

Agnes wandered back to her desk and sat down with a sigh.

"Slowly," she said. "Where we are in luck is that due to the nature of the houses in Norfolk, Cornwall and

Aberdeenshire, we already had sleeper cells in place as volunteers. Marjory has activated the volunteers, so they carry on as normal but are now briefed on what the mission is and the item we are looking for. They're paying extra attention to anything new, or out of place, in the rooms they have access to and any new faces 'back of house' as it were."

"What about the rooms they're not allowed in?" asked Delores.

"Using Armadillo's help, I've been able to get some of our people in on the payroll. Cleaners, housemaids, footmen and the odd butler. They've been finding some remarkable stuff but nothing that actually helps us."

"Not even on the stuff Armadillo claimed had gone missing? I think it was the silver jug, candlesticks some books and a rug."

"Blanket," said Agnes.

"That's it," said Delores. "Nothing on those?"

"Not yet, but not all areas have been searched yet. It's a case of slowly does it and to not draw attention to what they're actually doing."

"Well," said Delores, "it'll be interesting what the ladies come back with after their event at the police station. Let's see if there's anything in the report that matches anything he's told us so far. Gotta be honest, I *still* think it's a wind-up."

"It would be an impressive wind-up, if that were the case," admitted Agnes, "and if it was a wind-up then what on earth would he gain from it, but I agree an open mind is best. Anyway, Marjory mentioned the police station visit won't be until March next year. She tried to get in earlier, but due to staff shortages, the community liaison office has had to push their visit out, so unless there's a break in the case before then, we won't hear any more for a while."

Delores jumped as her phone bleeped. It was a reply from Ellen.

"Ellen says '29th of December at 6p.m. Can't do any quicker due to the extra bank holidays on the Monday and Tuesday but the 29th is the first day back.'"

"29th it is then," said Agnes, as Delores's phone bleeped again.

"She wants to know if we can tell her now who's been responsible for all this."

"I don't think that would be at all appropriate," said Agnes.

"Totally agree," said Delores, typing back a quick reply.

"Poor Santa," said Agnes looking at the image on the wanted board.

Twelve

Wednesday, 29th December 2021

On the brutally cold evening that was the 29th of December, the entire Crispin family – Charles, Ellen, Lizzie, Charlie, CC and even Karen Crispin – all gathered in the canteen of Crispin Crisps. None of them wanted to be there, but Ellen could be very persuasive at times and the family knew better than to refuse her when she was 'on one'.

One after the other they all traipsed in to find they were not alone. Already seated were Alice Alderman, Jason Sadler, Daniel Smythe, Lee Turner and Charles's PA, Anne Mayhew. All with a vested interest in finding out once and for all who was responsible for the year of hell and their reason why. Apart from an acknowledgement between them of 'evening' or 'hello' no other words were exchanged. The silence was only broken by the occasional crunch of a pack of Crispin Crisps being opened and consumed.

Also in the room and stood to one side were Agnes and Delores, who beckoned the family in and pointed to the chairs which had been laid out in a semicircle. As the family members took their seats, everyone realised that all the chairs in the semicircle were now taken which could only mean that no one else was expected.

Charles broke the silence, demanding to know why the hell they had been summoned.

"You're not the police," he said angrily to Agnes and Delores. "You have no right or authority to summon us here tonight."

"Sit down and be quiet, Charles," said a very determined Ellen. "I've told you already, that I'm not going on pretending anymore that everything's alright and ignoring what's been happening around us. I've had enough. I just want to know once and for all so we can end this tonight. *I* asked Agnes and Delores to look into this for me, so they have every right to be here, so we're all going to stay here until this is over. Do you understand?"

Charles was momentarily taken aback. He was used to Ellen going on about the incidents at home, but this was the first time he'd seen her lose it in public and in front of staff. Ellen stared into his eyes. "For me, Charles, stay here and listen for me." Before Charles could speak, Charlie butted in.

"I'm with Dad on this one. Those two..." pointing to Agnes and Delores, "have nothing. They're just two interfering busybodies in our family business. Well I'm not putting up with it tonight so I'm out of here."

"Sit down, Charlie," said Ellen in a very calm, yet determined forceful tone.

"Do as your mother says," sighed Charles, knowing better not to disagree with Ellen when she used 'that' tone of voice. "Your mother's right," he said, glancing at Ellen, sighing as he reached out and took her hands. Looking directly at Charlie he said, "This ends tonight. So sit down and shut up, whilst we listen to what the ladies have to tell us." Ellen gave Charles a weak but grateful loving smile, which he returned, squeezing her hands as Charlie returned to his seat glaring at them both.

Charles then looked over at Agnes and Delores. Truth be told, he didn't want to be here either but if they had to be, then he quickly wanted it over and done with.

"Get on with it," he said in a polite, yet slightly menacing tone.

Before either spoke, Agnes and Delores looked around those seated in the semicircle and then glanced back at one another. As Agnes began to speak, the crisp crunching from those in the semicircle slowly came to a stop.

"Whenever a crime is committed regardless of what that crime may be, the same three things are always considered." She looked over at Delores, who continued.

"Means. Motive. Opportunity."

"But," said Agnes, "that's not really right, is it? The order's all wrong. What it really should be is…"

"Motive. Means. Opportunity," said Delores. "Whoever committed the crime, had to have a reason for doing so, i.e. the 'motive'. Once you have the motive, you have the 'who' and once you have the 'who', the means and opportunity fall into place."

"Let's look at the facts," said Agnes. "Over the past year the factory has been targeted on many different occasions and in many different ways. Whether it's been the company's reputation or damage to vehicles or damage to machinery and now individual employees impacted, these are deliberate acts of malice."

"Incredible when you think about it," said Delores. "After all, Crispin Crisps is a well-loved local business. Long standing, loyal to the area and loyal to its employees. Anne – you even mentioned how well the company and the family looked after you last year after your brother died."

Anne nodded her head. A single tear ran down her face as the memories of those dark days came flooding back to her. She tried to muffle her sniffing as she said, "The family were wonderful to me at the most horrible time of my life. They gave me all the time I needed on full pay and never once asked when I was coming back. They looked after me."

"Well, of course we did," puffed Charles, "we're all family here."

Charlie snorted then glared at his father.

"I don't recall you being that nice to me when I had *my* run-in with the police. You didn't stick up for me then. Where was this 'family' then, Dad?"

"You were caught drunk driving, Charlie," said Charles. "Entirely different and you could have hurt someone. Quite frankly, the police were right to prosecute you and anyway, we paid your court fine and the fee for your safer driver's course. It's not like we abandoned you." Charles looked up at Delores.

"We are a family at Crispin Crisps, we may not be related to everyone, but we look after everyone. Whether they're blood relations or not."

"Which makes it even stranger that a company with

such a good reputation, to the point of giving all employees above-inflation wage rises this year, a generous holiday allowance, healthcare discounts, you name it, has been carefully and meticulously targeted. Your year of sabotage ending with Secret Santa—"

"—Satan Santa," interjected Agnes.

"Well quite," said Delores, "but the stakes have got higher now. Someone means business and as your people are now the targets, the game has to stop before someone really gets hurt."

The thought of this made Ellen shudder and tears fell from her eyes. The others in the semicircle had different reactions. Some in the group looked to their left and right, looking intently at everyone else to see how they reacted. Some just shifted uncomfortably in their chairs and some just stared down at the floor or straight ahead desperate not to make eye contact with anyone else.

"Hang on a minute," said Jason Sadler. "We're the only ones here so that means you think one of us is guilty."

"Oh no," said Agnes, "we don't 'think' it was one of you."

"We '*know*' it was one of you," said Delores.

"That's outrageous," snapped Lizzie. "How dare you even think it was me. I'm a *Crispin*! An actual member of this actual family. This lot…" - she paused and pointed to the others in the group - "fair enough, I wouldn't trust them in the slightest. But don't you dare accuse me."

"You '*know*', do you?" snarled Charlie, as if challenging Agnes and Delores to a duel. "Prove it. Go on, prove it. And I bet you can't." Charles looked at his adult children and quietly but firmly told them to 'sit down and shut the hell up'.

Jason asked again, "You really know who did it and seriously, legit one of us?"

"Afraid so," said Agnes.

"Well, could you please get on with it then," said Lee Turner, "because it's been a hell of a year and I for one am completely fed up with it all."

"No, wait a moment," interrupted Charles. "If, as you say, you can prove who did that, and it's someone sitting here now, why aren't Richard and Jayne here? Surely HR and Legal need to be involved?"

"We briefed them earlier," said Agnes. "They're in the building as well and will join us later." Although to be honest, Agnes wasn't entirely sure that Richard Coates fully grasped what they had told him and Jayne just before the others arrived. The more they explained, the louder his crisp munching became.

Both Charles and Ellen looked deflated at hearing that HR and Legal had been fully briefed. For Ellen, it meant that this was real; she hadn't been overreacting, and for Charles, it suddenly became clear to him that he should have taken Ellen's fears seriously much, much earlier. Looking at everyone in the semicircle, it hit them that someone sitting alongside them right now was who had been responsible for this horrible year.

"I want to know right now," demanded Alice Alderman, living up to her Miss Nasty reputation, "which one of this lot was responsible for my Secret Santa present. I don't care about anything else or anyone else. Tell me and tell me right now."

"No," Agnes said to her, "not yet." Alice started to lift herself up off the canteen chair as if she was about to launch an assault on someone. CC, who was sat next to her, grabbed her arm and mouthed the word 'sit' to her.

Delores picked up two files from a table behind her and gave one to Agnes, then turned back to face the group.

"Family," she said, "it's an interesting concept really. Blood family, work family, one big, happy family aren't you? But the thing with 'family' is that people have secrets. Some people have a past that they want to keep buried and some have a long-forgotten past which someone else is only too happy to dig up and share with others."

"But those secrets," continued Agnes, "can only stay buried for a finite amount of time. A careless word here, or a careless act there and suddenly those long-ago secrets come crashing through the door."

At that exact point, everyone in the canteen jumped out of their skins when the canteen doors crashed open and banged with alarming ferocity the walls from which they were hung.

"Sorry… sorry…" said a new voice. It was Richard closely followed by Jayne. "Have we missed much?" he asked.

Delores, having also turned pale and begun hyperventilating at the sudden entrance, managed to get out, "No, no, you're all good, we've only just started."

"Have you finished what you were working on?" asked Agnes.

"We have," said Jayne, indicating to a folder she was carrying.

Richard went over to the wall of crisps and grabbed a couple of packets before dragging a couple of chairs over to join the group; he couldn't have made more noise if he tried. Then, as if playing a child's party game, all those seated in the semicircle had to drag their chairs over a bit, shuffling along to make room for the additional two. Agnes whispered to Delores, "I kind of thought they'd sit over there where we had the two chairs ready at the back."

"I'm not convinced he's a details person," whispered back Delores.

"Frightening," was Agnes's reply as Richard proceeded to drop his pen which somehow then rolled under the chair next to him and continued rolling until it stopped under the chair of Charles. Richard saw the look on Charles's face and decided against asking him to pick the pen up for him so began rifling through his suit pockets for a spare. He mainly found sweet wrappers that did nothing to abate the noise emanating from him and nothing to reduce the increasing incandescent shade of red rage glaring from Charles's face.

"And he works in HR," muttered Agnes a lot more quietly than Richard could dream of.

"Doubly frightening," muttered Delores. "Too loud man… too loud, shush now."

When silence fell and Richard was eventually in receipt of a new pen, Delores continued.

"Family. But what actually is 'a family'? People… blood or otherwise, who are supposed to care about one another and do what's right."

Charlie tried and failed to suppress a snort of laughter.

"But you didn't do that, did you…?" said Agnes, just stopping short of naming the perpetrator. Instead, her eyes roamed across the semicircle looking at each person in turn. "Did you, Karen?" she finally said.

The room gasped, then lots of voices all at once.

"Karen... *Karen*... you?"

"Why?"

"What!"

"No!"

"Oh my God!" Although that came from Richard who had managed to knock over the bottle of water he'd brought in with him.

Everyone in the group turned to look at Karen. Karen herself looked shocked and stunned at the accusation. Slowly and quietly she said, "In case you hadn't noticed, I've been in Australia until two days ago. There is absolutely *no* way possible that I could be here sending emails, sabotaging the factory, leaking information or be in Secret Santa. I. Wasn't. Here. And if that's the quality of your so-called detecting skills then I suggest you stick to your day jobs."

"My sister's right," said Charles, "she's been in Oz all this time with her husband. I collected them both from the airport two days ago so I'm sorry, you've got this one wrong."

"The thing is though," said Agnes, "who mentioned leaks? You all know about the emails, the physical damage, the supplier relationship harm and Secret Santa, but we've never mentioned leaks."

"Don't be so stupid," said Karen. "They told me," pointing towards Charles and Ellen.

"No," said Ellen. "I don't even know about any leaks – did you, Charles?" Charles shook his head to indicate no.

"*They* told me!" said Karen getting quite flustered, now pointing at Charlie and Lizzie. "Over dinner last night."

Both Charlie and Lizzie shook their heads.

"I wasn't even at dinner last night," said Charlie.

"I was but like Mum I have no idea about any leaks," said Lizzie.

"What leaks, Agnes?" asked Ellen. "I really don't know about any leaks?"

"When we reviewed the timeline of events that had happened here, there were a few months when nothing was reported," said Agnes.

"But as it turned out, this wasn't quite right," continued Delores. "There were leaks sent out in October, but they never made it out into the public domain. They were sent to the same journalist who the original emails were sent to. She'd already got her fingers burnt by the false information in those emails, and even though this time the leaks came from an anonymous source, the style and layout were exactly the same, so she did nothing with them. They were kept on file but never saw the light of day."

"So, Karen," said Agnes. "The only other person who knew about the leaks was the 'leaker' and you're the only person who's mentioned them. No one in the family knew so no one could have told you."

Karen looked flustered. She tried to speak but nothing would come out. She stood up as if to leave but Agnes blocked her way. Sitting back down again, the look on her face changed from fluster and panic to cold, hard hate.

"Okay, yes," she said, "it was me and I don't regret a thing."

Charles looked shocked.

"Why, Karen? Why on earth would you do this?" Karen turned to face her brother.

"Why, dear brother? I'll tell you why. You know how hard Doug and I worked to set up a factory in Australia. We sunk everything into it heart and soul, but you never supported us. The staff kept wanting more money for fewer hours. The customers wanted cheaper and cheaper products, but suppliers kept putting up the prices. We did everything we could to keep going, but not once did you support us. It was your fault we failed, and it wasn't fair that the factory over here was doing so well. I'd had enough so you deserve everything that happened this year."

"Karen, that's just not true," said Charles. "We loaned you eight million pounds to set up, we gave you free licencing rights to the product names, we even sent out our department heads, but you didn't listen. You *wouldn't* listen. You wanted to do things your way, you kept saying. But even when the business was failing it didn't stop you from buying the big houses, the flash cars and going on expensive holidays, did it?"

"We had to do all of that," scoffed Karen. "People needed to know we ran a successful business and could afford to do so."

"But that's the point," said Charles, "you couldn't afford it. You used up all the money on your material wants and not investing in the factory. You kept asking for more and more money until the point came when we couldn't afford to prop you up. Your failure is entirely on you."

"Well, I can blame you and I do blame you," said Karen. "'Family,'" she said pointing to Delores, "it's what she said. But if this was a real family, you'd have looked after me. I am a Crispin. I deserve to have nice things." Karen slumped back in her chair, face glowing red with anger and hatred.

Charles shook his head; he looked deflated finding out it was his own sister who'd carried out these actions against them. How could she do this to them? Charles pondered for a few seconds then frowned, then thought again before saying out loud, "How did you do all of this? The physical sabotage and Secret Santa? You were in Australia so you must have had help. Tell me how and tell me who?"

Karen refused to answer, so Agnes did instead.

"I got hold of the emails received by the newspapers and banks that Karen had sent and compared them to the digital footprint in your IT systems. Not just the emails, but the code and the algorithms behind them. I was able to trace the transmissions from source to final destination. They were of course sent from a fake Crispin Crisps email account with the IP address spoofed multiple times to make it look like they were sent from here, but I back-tracked and broke down each IP address. You were very clever, Karen, with the IPs but eventually they led back to the original IP and right back to Karen's house in Australia. I was then able to remotely access the laptop." Agnes paused. "Seriously, people, if someone sends you an email to say you've won £100,000 and all you have to do is click on a link to claim it, just don't. Please, just don't and instead, step away from your keyboard. You have no idea what those links actually contain."

It was at this point that Richard from HR made a mental note that he probably ought to get his laptop checked out as he still hadn't heard back from those solicitors who'd sent him an email to say he'd inherited £150,000 from a great aunt in America. All they'd needed was his bank details to transfer the money, but he decided he really should chase them again as he'd heard nothing since giving them his details.

Shortly after this first mental note, Richard's inner voice suggested that he quickly check his bank balance on his mobile phone app just to see if the money had come in yet.

"Oh dear," he muttered to himself upon seeing the numbers displayed in the app. "Oh no, oh dear." For the balance was now -£31.05 and he had no idea what the single outgoing transaction of £15,101.00 was for. Richard then realised that everyone in the room was staring at him staring at his mobile phone. He put his left hand up as some form of apology and quickly put his phone back in his pocket. Agnes continued.

"When I was able to access Karen's computer, I found the original copies of all the emails. They were all set up with a delivery delay on them, so they arrived in the UK during our office hours. Like I said, you really need to get better protection software on your devices. It was too ridiculously easy to access your machines. I also found the emails Karen sent in October with the leaks in. More fake information about the company. She'd got desperate that none of the emails or sabotage earlier this year had caused any long-term damage, so she thought she'd try again."

"When we first mapped out this year's catalogue of sabotage, we noted that there were several months where no activity took place and wondered if it was relevant," said Delores, "and as you heard Agnes say earlier, it most definitely was."

"But I still don't understand," said Charles. "Karen was in Australia until two days ago."

"Charles, when you picked up Karen and Doug at the airport, where did you meet them?" asked Delores.

Charles thought briefly and then said, "The main concourse on Terminal 2."

"So you didn't see them coming in through arrivals?" asked Delores. Charles shook his head.

"Well, it would have been miraculous if you had," said Delores, "as they've been back in the UK for two months."

"Sorry, what?" said Charles. "They couldn't have been. I met them at the airport two days ago."

"One of my contacts arrived back in the UK on the same flight and particularly noticed Karen who'd made a fuss about everything on the very long flight," said Delores. "Karen complained about the meals, the drinks and the other passengers, she complained when she wanted a free upgrade to first class but was refused, complained about the turbulence and why the pilot couldn't rise above it. Karen couldn't have been more noticeable if she'd tried. Karen and Doug disembarked just in front of my contact who, like many people on holiday, took photos of absolutely everything to 'remember the memories'. They had photos of you both on the plane, at the airport and getting into a taxi. The latter photo taken because your behaviour had been so odd. We were able to trace the taxi so knew exactly where you were dropped off and where you've been living these past couple of months. So, Charles, I'm afraid the arrival and you collecting them was one big con." Charles still looked confused.

"But even if that's right, and I still don't understand how, it doesn't explain how she could do the physical damage inside the factory or in the yard or the Secret Santa."

"They were definitely in Australia until two months ago. But when they came back to the UK in October, on the video calls you had with them they either didn't put a background on, or they did a fake background and green-screen filter. That's one thing technology has definitely got better on are the filters. You had no reason to think they were anywhere else but in Australia. But yes, they've been back since October and staying in Norwich which was probably the biggest risk of all. I can even show you the flight manifests and airport CCTV of their actual arrival, if you'd like," said Agnes.

"But that doesn't explain how she could have done the physical damage or ruin the Secret Santa event?" said Charles.

"People," interrupted Ellen. "You hurt people; these people," pointing at those sitting in the canteen semicircle. "How could you do that to us?" Agnes looked at Ellen.

"Oh, she didn't do any of that."

"What?" said Charles and Ellen simultaneously.

"Oh for God's sake," murmured Charlie.

"Seriously?" gasped Lizzie.

Karen stared at Agnes.

"That's the only thing you and I agree on," she said. "Emails and leaks, yep, that was me and I'll never regret them, but I didn't do anything else. Whether you believe me or not, I really don't care."

"I'm afraid Karen's right about the latter," continued Agnes. "She didn't do the physical sabotage and she didn't do Secret Santa."

Delores took over. "We've already determined that every investigation comes down to motive, means and opportunity. Well, Karen definitely ticks the motive box for everything that's happened. Her incompetence to run any kind of business is evident – no financial or business skills yet completely failing to take any responsibility and putting the blame entirely on the family and wanting revenge. But that's completely down to her and Doug; just happy to blame everyone else. Jealousy of the family success here in the UK and wanting revenge. No bigger motive than that. As for means, a hundred percent, on the emails and the leaks; Karen had the insider knowledge and the software technology to mask being the sender of the emails. But until two months ago, she and Doug were genuinely in Australia. There's no possible way she had the means or the opportunity to do anything else."

"Then who the hell did?" said Charles in a surprisingly menacing tone.

"Well, this is where it all gets rather interesting," said Delores, glancing at the papers in her file. "Family," she said.

"Oh, not this again," said Daniel.

"Afraid so," said Delores. "All roads lead back to family. Your blood family, your work family, in many cases *you… we…* we all spend more time with our work family than we do with our blood family." Agnes picked up the explanation.

"Sometimes the lines can get blurred, and you forget which is which, especially when your work family is also your blood family. A third-generation family business, a male-line generational family business where the oldest son inherits the business. And it was beginning to annoy you, wasn't it…" Agnes paused and looked at CC but instead said, "Charlie? You're what… forty-one years old? Already older than your father and grandfather were when they took over the business."

"And your father," said Delores, pointing to Charles, "shows absolutely no sign of retiring. Which means there's no sign of you getting the gift of the top job yet, is there?" Agnes took over.

"A spoilt, arrogant, entitled, middle-aged man child is what more than one person we've spoken to, has called you. You got everything you asked for. Even your drink-driving conviction was hushed up. Everything you asked for, apart from the one thing you really wanted. The company."

"Damn right I want this company," sneered Charlie. "I'm going to drag it kicking and screaming into the twenty-first century. Automation, increased production, cheaper produced products means better profits. What's wrong with that?"

"People, Charlie, what about the people?" said Charles. "Our founding values as you well know are People, Product and Pride. We are nothing, nothing without our staff, our work family."

"You're stuck in the past, Dad; times have moved on. *You* need to move on and move out. It's my turn and I want it now." Ellen stared at Delores whilst Charlie was venting his anger.

"I was right, wasn't I?" she said quietly. "When I came to see you, I told you it was our son. I was right but I can't believe it, I don't want to believe it, but I was right. I felt so guilty, I hated myself for even thinking those thoughts but deep down I knew." Charles reached over to comfort his wife.

"Charlie is without doubt the most unpleasant individual I've ever had the misfortune to meet, Ellen, but he's not guilty. He didn't do any of this either," said Delores as kindly as she could whilst simultaneously destroying the character of Ellen's son. "Whilst he had the motive, and he had the opportunity, he's not clever enough to tick the means box."

"For God's sake," exploded Charles, "first it's Karen, then it's Charlie, now it's not Charlie. Absolute rot; I've never heard such rubbish."

Delores ignored Charles and continued.

"It comes down again to motive, means and opportunity. Without doubt, Charlie had a motive. He's desperate to get his hands on the company, take control, change everything and do it all his way but as we've heard, there's no sign of that happening any time soon. Charlie was getting desperate. But to his delight, the emails started going out bad-mouthing the company, the family business, questioning the financial stability under the current leadership. Then when the sabotage started, Charlie could not believe his luck. So yes, Ellen, when you confronted him, he didn't deny it. But I bet he didn't explicitly say it was him either, did he?"

Ellen thought about it, trying to recall all the confrontations she'd had with Charlie over the last year.

"He kept laughing at me. Each time he'd just laugh and say I had no idea what he was capable of and that we should start to take notice of him and let him take over. But… " Ellen paused. "No, you're right, thinking about it, he never actually said it was him."

"He gave the same responses to us when we were

asking him about the events of the last twelve months," said Agnes. "Oh, he's more than happy to take the credit but he was simply not capable of actually carrying out the sabotage. But in many ways, Charlie also became the opportunity for the person who did."

"They both have the same motive," said Delores, "a *big* motive tick. But as you've heard, the emails and failed leaks were Karen but neither she nor Charlie was responsible for anything else. He's all mouth and no action so although he ticks the motive box, he doesn't tick means or opportunity. None of this is down to him as much as he'd like to make you think otherwise."

Ellen looked up at Agnes and then over to Delores.

"Well, if Karen did the leaking and the emails, but Charlie didn't do anything, who did?"

"There was a brief moment when we thought Alice and CC were involved in all the incidents this year," said Agnes.

"*What!*" spluttered an up-until-now very quiet CC.

"You're joking, right!" snapped Alice.

"Far from it, Alice," said Agnes. "Deadly serious."

"Absolute rubbish," said Alice. "Call yourselves investigators? You couldn't investigate your way out of a paper bag. Pathetic."

"Why on earth did you think I had anything to do with this?" asked a more reasonable CC. "I can assure everyone in this room right now that it was not me."

"Stupid witches," said Alice. "I'm only here because I want to know who gave me my stupid present and I'd be very careful if I was you accusing me of something I didn't do."

"Alice," said Delores, trying her hardest to remain

polite, "if you'd listen properly, you'd have heard the words 'brief moment' and 'thought'. Both of you were considered but not for long."

"Why did you even think it was us?" asked CC.

"Well, that's on Alice," said Agnes. "She had a calendar in her desk with the dates circled that the emails went out and your initials next to them."

"How the hell do you know what's in my desk?" Alice almost yelled. Agnes ignored her question.

"We considered," said Delores, "that you and Alice were working together, and that you, CC, were jealous as the younger brother who didn't inherit the business, and that you wanted to cause trouble for Charles."

"Please be under no illusion," said CC, "that I ever wanted to inherit the business. Yes, I am a Crispin and yes, this business will always be my family business, but I have never, *ever* wanted to be in control."

"Agreed," said Delores. "We did some more digging on Alice and found that what she'd noted was nothing to do with you, CC."

"How dare you go through my private effects," said Alice. "I could sue you."

"No, Alice, you can't," Jayne Johns suddenly piped up. "Your desk and its contents are company assets. Anything personal, like your handbag and what's in it belongs to you, but any stationery is ours."

"Alice was actually attending interviews on these days, first and second interviews," said Agnes, "but as you can see by the fact she's still here," Agnes's inner voice butted in 'sadly' before her outer voice continued, "…she was never offered the role she went for."

"How do you know?" said Alice. "Maybe I turned it down. Maybe I was too good for them."

"We saw the rejection email you got from them, Alice. Why you used your work email, who knows, but thank you for doing so because it was a huge help," said Agnes. Alice glared at Agnes then Delores.

"'CC' didn't mean you," said Delores to CC, "it stood for Cunningham Cars so another coincidence but one that ruled both of you out."

"Good," said CC, "because it wasn't me. It was not me... I've got nothing to do with any of this," he said to the group, then Charles, then Ellen.

"So we're back to square one again," said Charles before saying very slowly and deliberately, "Who... was... it?"

For a brief moment, neither Agnes nor Delores said anything. It could only have been a few seconds, but in that room with these people, it felt like hours. Delores looked at everyone in the canteen, making uncomfortable eye contact with each of them.

"This person ticks all the boxes: motive, means and opportunity. Let's start with motive, because it's exactly the same as Karen and Charlie. Yet again, it all boils down to family jealousy."

As Delores spoke, Agnes slowly walked over to where Ellen was sitting. Looking straight into her eyes, Agnes quietly said, "And yet again, the cause of all this strife, Charles, is family. A family who in public embodies all that is good within a family business. A family who you still believe in and still think is fundamentally good. But it's not quite true." Ellen's face took on a pale pallor as Agnes spoke, and her eyes bored into hers. Ellen began to shake uncontrollably. Agnes continued, still staring at Ellen.

"It's not true, is it…" Agnes suddenly looked to her left, "…Lizzie?"

The room gasped once more and everyone turned to look at Lizzie, who was clearly not expecting to be called out. Richard from HR jumped and knocked his water over again.

"What?" shrieked Lizzie. "How dare you? I've already told you, I'm a *Crispin*, an actual member of the family. I've dedicated my life to this family and our business. There's no way in hell I'd do anything to damage either. It's my life." Charles stood up abruptly.

"You'd better have a damn good explanation," he said angrily to Agnes and Delores. "This is just too crazy to be true."

"Let them carry on and sit back down," Ellen said back to him. "I said this ends tonight so let them carry on and get this over and done with." Charles reluctantly sat down, glaring first at his wife, then Agnes, then Delores, then Charlie, then Lizzie, then CC, then Karen. Charles was getting increasingly annoyed with his entire family and began to wonder if he should jack it all in right now and spend the rest of his days on his boat sailing the broads and enjoying the peace and quiet and more importantly, no family.

"The business is your life, Lizzie. I completely agree with you. You live, breathe and sleep this business. Everything you do, you do for the good of the business whilst upholding those long-held values of People, Pride and Product. This business, this factory, is who you are. It's in your soul," said Agnes, "and it's exactly why you did all the things you did. Your motive was to protect the factory, protect the people, protect the product, protect the future."

"Protect it from who?" interrupted Charles. "Seems to me if she did these things then the factory wouldn't have a future."

"Exactly the point," said Agnes. Agnes looked back at Lizzie. "Lizzie's love for the business is all consuming, but she also worries deeply about the future. And yes, yet again, we're back to the theme of family. And the motive in this case is love and protection. Charles, you're the third-generation Crispin to run the family business and you uphold those values your grandfather held so dear, and you've also made it clear that you'll uphold the legal foundation of the business – which some people might think a little old-fashioned in this day and age–" at this point, Agnes looked at Jayne Johns, Legal Director, who nodded back, "that the oldest son inherits the business either through retirement, illness or even death of the previous incumbent. Charlie's made it very clear he wants to do things his way, which means modernising the business, replacing people with machines, and he's very much motivated by money, rather like his aunt; the more of it, the better."

"Still don't see what's wrong with that," interrupted Charlie. "If this business is to survive, we need to make more money. People are the most expensive expenditure after machinery, so with fewer people we immediately start to make more money. No more massive salary bills, holiday pay or pensions, no more wasting money on keeping employees happy. Ideally, a fully automated factory with the bare minimum needed just to maintain it, subcontracted to a third party, and customers sending in their own trucks for pickups. Then I can guarantee this business will keep going into the future and beyond."

"That's the point, you total idiot," snarled Lizzie to Charlie. "You couldn't give a toss about the founding principles of this business… *our* business, it's all about the people here, the products we make and the pride we take in doing this. None of that means anything to you and given the opportunity, you'll destroy it if you get your way. The reputation of our business will go down the toilet and no one will want to supply us or buy from us. You want to buy cheap and sell high, but it just won't work. You'll put generations of staff from the same families out of work, all so you can make a quick buck. You'll destroy it all, Charlie."

Charlie clearly disagreed with his sister, vehemently shaking his head at everything she said.

"If you think about the sabotage, whether it was supplier or customer impacting, the damage in the factory and to the transport, these are all things linked to Lizzie in her role as Supply Chain Director. Who better to disrupt the supply chain than the supply chain director herself?" said Delores. "She had unfettered access to the machinery and you've no CCTV in the factory or the yard because the business is built on the overriding goodwill and trust that you think the employees have here with you, and even if Lizzie was seen, no one would have reason to question why she was on the factory floor or out in the yard. It's the perfect cover."

"The trust you have in your people, Charles," said

Agnes, "is so high, so impenetrable, that no one thinks there's any reason to doubt the staff, no reason why any of them would go out of their way to harm the business. And maybe you're right to think the best of your employees considering that the person responsible is not just a director but a member of the family too."

"Lizzie knew that suspicion would fall on Charlie. He's made no effort not to deny he wants control and every effort to tell everyone what changes he'd make and as you're all aware, none of his plans fit in with the founding ethos of the family business. Charlie, without realising, played into Lizzie's hands. Every time an accusation came his way, he lapped up the attention and wound you all up even more with his baseless threats. He added to the opportunity that Lizzie had by taking the blame. Lizzie thought you'd…" Delores pointed to Charles and Ellen, "… agree he couldn't be trusted and that you'd never allow him to inherit the business which you would instead give to her. But Charles's refusal to take these events seriously and his refusal not to review how the business was inherited just infuriated Lizzie even more. So each time she upped her game to try and get your attention."

Charles looked at his daughter, horrified and disgusted.

"This was you, Lizzie, you?" Charles still struggled to believe the words he was saying. "Why didn't you come and talk to me?"

"You still have no idea, do you?" said Lizzie. "It's for the exact reasons they've just said. You always take his side. All my life, all his life, you've given him everything; let him get away with everything. You spoil him even when he's been an absolute vile pig – you always give in to him. Even if I'd have come to you to talk about him and about the future, you'd have patted me on the head and sent me on my merry way, just like you did with Mum every time she tried to talk to you about what's been going on this year. So yes, I came up with a plan to force your hand, but it was to protect the business, protect our people and protect our legacy. I tried to get you to see sense, but he'll win yet again."

"As you can see, it's a very clear *motive* in Lizzie's own words," said Agnes.

"So let's move onto *means*," said Delores. "As Supply Chain Director, Lizzie had access to all customer orders, suppliers and supplies, machinery inside the factory and the trucks outside. You could come and go as you pleased, and no one would bat an eyelid to see you on the factory floor or out in the yard."

"Which leaves us with *opportunity*," said Agnes. "Charlie was continually accused of the events, and you made full use of that opportunity to deflect your acts on him. You were able to use the shared supply chain email address, but you didn't sign them. They just went out on the auto signature of the team, 'Crispin Crisps, Supply Chain'. The emails were all sent from your laptop, either early in the day or late in the evening. Never when any other supply chain staff were in, but always sent when Charlie was in."

"But how did you know they were from me?" asked Lizzie. "You said yourself they weren't signed."

"Simple," said Agnes, "everyone has their own writing style, and most of the time no one's aware of their style especially when communicating electronically, but there's always a rhythm or a pattern or certain words and phrases used. Something that sets one person's tone of email apart from someone else's."

Lizzie looked confused.

"I still don't know, though, how you can prove it was me?"

"For the simple reason that you're the only person in the office who sends emails in Calibri font and everyone else uses the pre-set Arial. They look very similar if you're not paying attention but put them together and there's a clear difference."

"Although there is one person who uses Comic Sans," said Delores, "in itself a sackable offence, surely?"

Richard from HR knew not to make eye contact with anyone at this point and made yet another mental note to change his font.

"Your font, Lizzie, it was your font that gave you away," said Agnes.

"Now let's think about the tampering of the machines and how you did that," said Delores. "Glue in the potato peeler and slicer, mixed-up seasoning labels, missing forklift keys, loose bolts on the production lines. No one would ever question why the supply chain director was on the shop floor, would they? After all, it's what you Crispins do... roll up your sleeves and get involved. Obvs not you, Charlie."

"Lizzie, you had the motive, the means and the opportunity," said Agnes.

"And I still don't see how you can prove it was me on the shop floor or in the transport yard doing these things. You said yourself there's no CCTV."

"Absolutely, Lizzie, I agree there's no CCTV in the factory," said Delores, "however, what you failed to take into account when slashing the tyres in the yard is that there's CCTV overlooking the main road outside. For years, companies have complained about speeding traffic and the council finally installed speed cameras and traffic cams late last year. Agnes was able to access the footage and travel back in time and guess what? She saw you. Quite simply, Lizzie, you're caught on camera."

Lizzie pursed her lips, knowing full well she couldn't deny it any longer.

"Once I saw you on the footage," said Agnes, "you became number one suspect for the damage inside the factory as well. So I got a metal detectorist friend to come in and search the grounds. He quickly found the missing keys and the knife you used in one of the prickly bushes that edge the transport yard, along with a pot of glue you'd clearly used on the machinery. Maybe you thought no one would ever look that closely in the bushes but you were wrong."

"But I wiped everything clean like they do on TV and anyway, a fingerprint wouldn't last that long," said Lizzie.

"A fingerprint on a smooth surface can last a very long time," said Delores, "and not only did you leave a partial print but luckily for us, the prickly bush actually protected everything from the elements as well." Lizzie shook her head. She thought she'd been so careful to hide her actions but now there was nowhere to hide.

"Do you remember when Agnes and I came in on your Christmas bazaar day? You were offered free tea and biscuits? The ladies who were serving kept back the paper cups and Agnes compared your fingerprints from the cup to everything we recovered, and they matched." Delores kept quiet that her and Agnes had also done a sweep of the offices and factory on the day before the bazaar and also gathered a whole host of fingerprints as well.

"Now, you could rightly argue that as Supply Chain Director you have every right to be in the transport tard," said Agnes, "but why would a supply chain director's fingerprints be all over a knife, some keys and a pot of glue – all of which without doubt linked to the sabotage?"

"Motive," said Delores.

"Tick," said Agnes.

"Means," said Delores.

"Tick," said Agnes.

"Opportunity," said Delores.

"Tick," said Agnes.

"Proof," said Delores.

"Tick," said Agnes.

Lizzie turned to her parents; she tried in vain to justify her actions.

"I did it to protect everyone. Don't you get it?"

Charles looked straight at her.

"All I've learnt tonight, Lizzie, is that I've a sister and a daughter who have both tried to destroy the family business and a son who, given half the chance, will finish the job. It's not been the best of nights, so probably best if you shut the hell up."

Charlie opened his mouth to give his view on the matter as well; judging by the look on his face he was clearly delighted his sister and his aunt were guilty, but before he got a chance to speak, Charles looked at him and said, "That goes for you too."

Ellen looked at Delores.

"My head is whirring, it's just so much to take in and part of me regrets ever wanting to find out." Ellen then looked at Charles. "Maybe I should have kept quiet," she said to him. "I'm so sorry."

"No," he replied, shaking his head, "you did the right thing, and I was a fool not to have listened to you over these past few months. Quite what we do next I have no idea, but I'm assuming Jayne and Richard have a plan, seeing as they were told first."

Jayne and Richard nodded their heads. Richard looked over at Agnes, who discreetly nodded her head back to him. Richard then spoke. "About that plan, well I'm afraid you're not out of the woods just yet."

Before Charles could say anything, Jason Sadler piped up and said, "What I don't understand, Lizzie, is that you say you did this to protect the business and protect the people but what have you got against me? Or Alice or Daniel or Lee? We all had horrible Secret Santa gifts and I get now why you wanted your father to suffer with his and why you gave yourself a nasty present, so you didn't stand out. But what have I ever done to you?"

Alice also stared at Lizzie. "I agree. What have I ever done to you? We've always got on well and I can't think of one thing I've done to offend you – I've never offended anyone here. Same as Jason, what have I ever done to you?" Delores had to react very quickly to stifle a snort, disguising it as a cough, and return her flared nostrils back to half mast at Alice's comment. She'd already been banned by Agnes from lacing Alice's chair with itching powder which she thought was very unjust given Alice's reputation as Miss Nasty.

Daniel nodded in agreement with Alice. "I'm with them. There's never been any beef between us, Lizzie, so why me?"

Lee also spoke up. "Same here. If, as you claim, Lizzie, you were protecting the 'people', why the hell have you gone after the very people you think you're protecting? It doesn't make sense."

"The problem," said Agnes, "the problem is... well, actually, Lizzie, do you want to tell them?"

This surprised the group. What more could Lizzie possibly tell them? Lizzie took a breath.

"Well, if you insist," she said in a somewhat nasty tone.

"I do," said Agnes.

"Suit yourself," said Lizzie who proceeded to calmly look around the group. "I'm not Secret Santa."

There was a mixture of reactions in the room. Charlie roared out loud with laughter. Charles and Ellen looked even more horrified than they thought was possible a mere few seconds earlier. Karen and CC looked confused and impressed at the revelation and Alice, Daniel, Lee and Jason just looked completely lost.

Lizzie repeated her words. "I'm not Secret Santa."

"That's it," said Ellen, "I can't take any more of this." She stood up and started to make her way to the doors. "I need some air." Delores swiftly moved to block Ellen's exit.

"No," said Delores to her. "I know it's been a rough evening but please sit back down. This ends tonight, and I promise you this is the final piece of the puzzle."

As Ellen reluctantly sat back down a clearly rattled Charles said, "Let's get this right again, shall we? A sister sending inflammatory emails and failed attempts at malicious leaking. A daughter sabotaging the business. An incompetent son incapable of opening a bag of crisps let alone running a business. And now you're telling me there's someone else involved? Is there anyone here not involved? Incredible… absolutely incredible. So why don't you get on with it then, come on let's hear it, let's finish off this evening from hell, shall we?"

Delores and Agnes paused, gathering their thoughts on how they were about to turn Secret Santa into less of a Secret and just plain old Santa. Agnes took a deep breath and started.

"As has been the theme with the previous current guilty parties, we're still looking at 'family' as the motivation in Secret Santa. But layered on top of that is revenge, and despair *and*, I think deep-seated sadness."

"I'm afraid for a business that has 'people' as a founding principle, it seems a lot of the people here may not necessarily be the nicest of people," said Delores, "and yes, you have your HR policies in place…"

At this point Agnes glanced over at Richard who was now on his fourth packet of crisps and then over to Charles who was sitting there with a face like thunder glaring at Richard. "Such as they are,' she muttered before Delores continued.

"…But it would appear that even if someone tried to raise a concern or report a problem, it's swept under the carpet. The Secret Santa Slayer felt they had no choice after not being taken seriously after, well, I'll be honest, years of festering, and so they snapped. The six of you who received gifts were deliberately targeted by the same person. Some of you were selected because you shared a past history with the slayer and that history manifested itself whilst here at Crispin Crisps and for some of you, it was simply down to more recent events."

"So we can definitely tick the motive box," said Agnes. "Revenge, despair, sadness and family. So let's look at means next. Who had the means, let alone the opportunity, to swap out your original gifts for these slightly less festive ones?" Alice Alderman opened her mouth to ask Agnes a question, but Agnes pre-empted her. "And yes, we do know the gifts were swapped. We've spoken to all the original gift givers who picked your names from the Santa hat," said Agnes pointing in a smooth movement to all the victims, "and all of them can prove they bought you something different, so yes, you were definitely targeted, and your gifts were swapped out."

"This time round though, it's actually *motive, opportunity* and *means*," said Delores. "Once the slayer realised how easy the opportunity was to make the swaps, the means became the easy part. Let's look at the facts as we know them. Every year Crispin Crisps holds a Secret Santa event for the employees. Not everyone takes part, but those who do put their names into the Santa hat in the canteen. After the closing date has passed, each person who put their name in the hat then pulls a name out and purchases a gift (with only a small monetary value) then wraps it up, labels the gift and places it in the meeting room right next to this very canteen."

"On the day of the gift opening," continued Agnes, "the gifts are moved from the meeting room to the canteen well before 8a.m. But unlike previous events, this time round, six of you received gifts which weren't that nice. Some cruel, some with nasty side effects. Lizzie, the lipstick that burnt your lips; Charles a jigsaw with a potentially threatening message on it; Daniel, the laxative-laced chocolates; Jason an exploding pen." At this point, Jason looked down at his still-blue ink-stained hand and tried to hide behind his back. "Alice, talcum powder filled with a considerable amount of itching powder. And Lee, boiled sweets which made your mouth bleed. Your original gifts were disposed of, but the labels retained and reattached to your new presents. We spoke to all of the original 'gifters' and they told us what they had purchased and wrapped up for you. Some still had the receipt, but they were very clear in what they bought you, from where and when."

"So this time round, revenge plays a major part in the motive. And the opportunity is clear – the gifts were all left unattended overnight before the big day so at least a twelve-hour window to swap them over."

"So that leaves us with the *means*."

"No," said Jason, "please just stop. I don't care about the means, just the who," said Jason. "All I want to know is who did this and why. I don't care how they did it, just who and why."

"We're getting there, Jason. Just a few more minutes, please," said Delores.

"The *means* is actually the simplest of them all. Itching powder, laxative-containing chocolates, blood sweets, burning lipsticks and an exploding pen are all items that you can buy from a joke shop. And that's exactly what the slayer did. And as for the jigsaw, well, you can buy a personalised gift from lots of different websites. No dodgy dealing, no dodgy websites, no specialist knowledge.

Anyone in this room could have done so. And that's exactly what one of you did," said Agnes.

"As part of our investigation, we looked at every act of sabotage that had happened earlier in the year," said Delores, "and we found *coincidences* where you could link the Secret Santa victims to each act of sabotage."

"But," said Agnes, "whilst it was Lizzie who carried out the sabotage, she wasn't involved in Secret Santa, so the coincidences were just that… coincidences. It meant there had to be another reason why you were targeted and no one else. But why?"

"When Lizzie, Alice, Jason, Lee and Daniel opened their gifts, they quickly discovered the side effects, but you, Charles, well, no side effects, just a very strange message which you didn't understand," said Delores.

"Still don't," said Charles.

"The slayer thought they'd covered their tracks completely. After all, your Secret Santa event was some weeks ago, but what they didn't take into account was Ellen," said Agnes.

Everyone glanced over at Ellen. "After nearly eleven months of bad luck, bad press and sabotage, Ellen was pretty paranoid. So when she realised that Secret Santa had been another act of sabotage, she quietly retrieved all the packaging without any of you knowing and brought it to us."

"Agnes ran some tests," said Delores, "and found that on all the other gifts there were multiple fingerprints, all over the wrapping paper and the labels, many sets of fingerprints as you'd expect from the sheer number of people who touched the items. But on your six gifts, it was only the label which had multiple prints on it. We had the list of who took part in this year's event, and we know from the six of you who you chose gifts for. Using the prints we were able to work out on the other gifts, who gave which gift to whom."

"But imagine my surprise," said Agnes, "when I found there were only two sets of prints on the wrapping paper. To start off with we also considered that each of you received a gift from someone who was playing a joke on you, but they ended up taking it a bit too far. But once I found that the wrapping paper had just two sets of prints on it, and one set matched all six items, then it became obvious that your original gifts from your original 'gifters' had been removed and the same person had targeted you all with very deliberate gifts. When we cross-matched the prints and found out who it was, we also realised it was the one person who, right from the start, didn't try to hide it. They blatantly and openly told us – told everyone – it was them. No doubt whatsoever, and yet no one, not you, not even we, realised that the truth had been told in plain sight. Hell, we even noted what they said to us in our files, but we didn't pay any attention to what they said."

Once more everyone seated turned to Charlie, the one person who happily and willingly took credit for the emails and the sabotage. The same person who threatened more to come if he wasn't taken seriously.

"Entertaining, isn't it!" he said with a grin on his face.

"Enough!" snapped Charles. "Are you finally telling me that this time it was Charlie?" Agnes didn't directly answer Charles's question.

"Maybe we should let the slayer explain for themselves,"

said Agnes. Delores looked round at all of the faces staring back at her in the semicircle.

"We're waiting," she said. No one spoke. "Still waiting." Silence continued so Delores carried on.

"This is your last chance. Take back a bit of dignity and come clean."

Agnes and Delores also stared at Charlie whilst the rest of the group sat in deafening silence. Ellen gave a gasp.

"Charlie. I knew it." Charlie remained silent with his grin getting bigger.

"No. Not Charlie," said Agnes, much to Charlie's disgust and Ellen's relief. "He may have spent all year winding you up and leading you on a merry dance to make you think it was him, but it wasn't."

"Is this true?" asked Ellen looking at Charlie. Charlie gave a grin and shrugged his shoulders before saying, "Okay so I was happy to take the blame for everything and wind you all up but if you really, really want to know… this wasn't me either. Soz." Ellen looked back at Delores who nodded.

"He's right. None of these items had Charlie's fingerprints on. The slayer isn't Charlie."

"So who was it?" asked Charles in despair.

"Well, there's only one thing for it," said Delores suddenly turning with Agnes to face a different direction. "You leave us no choice… one last chance… no? Okay…" they pivoted direction again, "the floor is yours, Anne."

The room gasped. Anne??? Anne Mayhew??? Lifelong employee and Charles's PA. Quiet, unassuming, hardworking, loyal Anne?

"Oh, come on now," said Charles, "I've never heard

such utter nonsense. There's no way this was Anne, she just wouldn't do this. Charlie, yes, completely agree he'd do it but not Anne."

"So sorry, Father dearest," said Charlie, "still not me."

"But Anne would, and Anne did," said Agnes. "She told us right at the start and I quote, 'I did it'… how she planned Secret Santa every year, how she organised everything including how she moved the gifts to the canteen, how she was the one who dressed as an elf every year and gave them out and how she tidied up the mess afterwards. *Motive…* tick… *Means…* tick…*Opportunity…* tick."

"No! This makes no sense," said Ellen, "this can't be Anne. Sorry, Delores and Agnes, you're wrong on this one. One hundred percent wrong."

"I wish we were, Ellen, but we're not," said Delores. "Do you remember when Agnes and I took on this case for you? We told you that if we accepted, there's a risk we'd find out information that the person asking for help – and that would be you – might not want to know? Well, it's our duty to tell you everything now, whether you like it or not."

Everyone by now was looking at Anne who was looking quite flushed as she protested her innocence.

"You're mad… it wasn't me; it could have been anyone swapping out presents. Everyone knows the timings and when I move the gifts in here."

"Except it was you, Anne, and we can prove it," said Delores.

"Rubbish," said Anne.

"Exactly that, Anne – rubbish," said Agnes. "The wrapping paper you threw in the rubbish bins was your undoing."

"I have to agree with Anne," said Charles, "this just isn't her. What possible reason do you have to think otherwise?"

"Fingerprints," said Delores. "Exactly the same way we could tie Lizzie to the sabotage."

"The wrapping paper that Anne used for your presents only had two sets of fingerprints on them," said Agnes. "Ellen had the foresight to use gloves when she retrieved the paper so as not to contaminate anything and when we compared the prints on the paper to the prints we took off the cups you used at the bazaar we were able to match the prints to the receiver of the gift and the Secret Santa Slayer… which, yes, I'm afraid is Anne." Agnes looked round at the others in the group. "She told us as much on the day of the bazaar… 'I did it, it was me' were the exact words she said."

Anne looked at Agnes.

"You're not forensic investigators though. You can't possibly match up fingerprints."

"Firstly, yes we can, and secondly, anyone can match fingerprints if they look closely enough," said Delores.

"Anne, it's easy to lift someone's prints. A quick Internet search will show you how if you don't already know and if you look at those prints under a microscope or even use a high-resolution camera to take a photo and create a really large image, the level of detail you can see is incredible. You'll all know that fingerprints are unique to every single individual and not even identical twins would match. So all we needed was a set of clear images and then to look for the same matches that a forensic investigator would," said Agnes.

"It's quite simple," said Delores. "If you all look at your fingertips…" everyone looked at their fingers at this instruction, "you'll see the patterns that are unique to you. Well, those pattens can officially be broken down into sections called amongst other things, lakes, spurs, forks, ridge ends, snail shells and arches. All unique to you. All we needed to do was compare one image against the other and look for where those patterns matched. With both Lizzie for the sabotage and Anne for Secret Santa, we were able to match enough markers to make a positive ID."

"And quite frankly, Anne," said Agnes, "even though, as you say, we may not be professional forensic investigators, it doesn't take a genius to see that your right-hand middle fingertip still has a deep scar from a recent cut."

Anne subconsciously hid her finger; she'd accidentally cut herself on a razor blade when she put her hand in her toiletries bag back in November. It was a long cut, at least 3cm and it went deep. So much blood had poured out at the time she'd needed to have stitches. And although the wound had now healed, a thick scar was very much still visible.

"Even if you don't want to believe we could match your unique pattern," said Agnes, "your scar gave you away as it showed up as clearly as you sat before us now on the prints we lifted."

Anne realised she couldn't argue her way out of this one.

"So let's start with Jason, shall we, Anne?" asked Delores. "His gift was the only one not linked to the factory. Maybe you'd like to tell him and everyone else why?"

Anne looked up then over at Jason. "You don't remember me, do you?" she asked.

Jason frowned and shook his head. "I know you've been here longer than me, but we've never been in the same team. Apart from working at the same place, I have no idea where you think we've met before."

"It was secondary school," said Anne finding her voice. "We were in the same year."

Jason shook his head. "So were a lot of kids, but I have no idea if you were there or not."

"Oh, I was there," said Anne. "Mr Powell's English class. All the way from starting secondary school right through to GCSE in the same class as you."

Jason still couldn't remember Anne. He sat there making an *I don't know* shrugging gesture.

"And?" he said. "Even if we were there at the same time, I have absolutely no memory of you."

"You were a nasty piece of work at school," said Anne, "bullying anyone who wouldn't join your gang, terrorising others who did and forcing them to do what you wanted."

"That was a long time ago," said Jason, looking flustered at his schoolboy behaviour. "I'm sure lots of us did a lot of things back then that we wouldn't do now."

"It might have been a long time ago to you, but those of us you bullied will never forget. You thought so little of us then, didn't you? Not even memories worth remembering now. But I remember. I remember you blackmailing me to write your homework essays. I was petrified of you, scared that if I wrote something which you got bad marks for you'd take it out on me."

"We were just kids," said Jason, "just kids being kids. You should've got a grip and moved on by now."

"Bullied kids have long memories," said Anne. "I hated writing your essays, I hated every word I wrote, and I hated every blue pen I used to write with. I hated you then and I hate you now. I thought I could ignore my feelings about you and I did for such a long time, but then, I heard you teasing someone in your team for their 'bad handwriting', so what better gift for you than a pen that explodes and leaves you permanently stained like you left me."

Jason looked shocked; he couldn't believe that a non-entity from his past could hold a grudge for so long. Facing Charles he said, "She's your employee; you'd better do something about her."

"One down, five to go," said Agnes before Charles could speak. "Let's move on to everyone else as you're all connected to the factory. Anne, why don't you tell us about Alice?"

"Yes, poor little Anne," sneered Alice. "Let's hear what you think I've done to deserve this," she said, pointing to her still itchy-red skin. "I gave you your first job here. You'd be nothing without me and the chance I gave you, and this is how you repay me?"

Anne looked at Alice. "Yes, you were my first line manager, the person who was the biggest influence in my whole working life. I was so excited to start working here, really looking forward to learning my job, meeting and making new friends, being part of a team. But you did nothing but make me feel like I was a nuisance. You made it clear you objected having to train me and you never answered any of my questions, oh, but you were always full of praise when senior management came round. Any ideas I had which were good, you took, but any time I got something wrong you took pleasure in mocking me. You made my skin crawl, so I thought I'd make yours crawl instead and there's nothing better than itching powder for that. So now you know just how you made me feel."

"I wish I'd never offered you the job," sniped Alice.

"Too late now, eh?" sniped back Anne, relieved that at last she was able to get her feelings off her chest.

"Two down, four to go," said Agnes, before Alice could reply. "How about Daniel next?"

"Yeah, come on," said Daniel, "what the hell did I do to you to deserve those disgusting chocolates?"

"That's easy," said Anne. "When I had the misfortune of being in *her* team," indicating towards Alice, "I found myself in need of some medical treatment. It was a little bit embarrassing, so I only told my manager. Clearly, she told you though, and every time our paths crossed you made sly comments, or you'd put your hand under your armpit to make joke noises. Or you'd shove things up your hi-vis jacket and keep saying 'I'm bloated, I'm bloated'. I had a twisted lower bowel, you moron, which caused me all sorts of pain and physical issues. It wasn't nice then and it's not nice now, so I thought I'd share those experiences with you."

Daniel clutched his stomach as the psychosomatic pain of searing stomach ache came back again. As a well-known chocolate lover, he'd wolfed down the entire pack of chocolates he'd been given within seconds. He didn't share them with anyone. The laxative effects were quick, explosive and left tears in his eyes. Images and sounds he'd never forget.

"Well, that's three down and three to go," said Delores. "Tell us about Lee."

"Yes, Anne," said Lee, somewhat sarcastically, "tell me about me. I've been sat here trying to think what you think I've done, and I can't come up with a damn thing. I remember you did a secondment in my team and from what I recall, you did quite well, but you went back to your original job and that's been the only time we've crossed paths."

Anne twisted sideways to be able to look at Lee. "You're one of the company's first aiders. The 'first on hand' if needed and you run the training courses."

"So what?" said Lee. "Surely you can't be jealous of that?"

"I went to one of your courses as part of our learning-at-work days."

"We did one of those as well at the agency," interrupted Agnes.

"Neither the time nor place," said Delores, briefly reliving her time in the surveillance van, when a car backfired, and her mug of chicken soup enrobed her keyboard and monitor in a moist but sticky creamy yellow undercoat. "Carry on, Anne."

"When I did the course, you were meant to be showing us how to deal with serious cuts. There are some very sharp bits of kit on the factory floor and if someone hurts themselves, we all need to know what to do."

"Is that what you didn't like?" asked Lee. "I don't get it, it's my job. Everyone knowing a bit of first aid could save a life. What's your problem?"

"You used real blood. I volunteered to go first but

you deliberately sprayed me with the stuff which made the others in the group roar with laughter at me. It was a horrible thing to do."

Lee shrugged. "It was just pig's blood, that's all. Made it look realistic."

"You just stood there and laughed along with everyone else whilst still trying to spray more at me. I was the only person you did that to; everyone else had fake blood. So when I saw the sweets, I thought of you. The moment you crunched them, they released that gooey red blood-like gel into your mouth. It looked even better than I'd imagined when you ate them. Blood pouring from your mouth. Now you know how I felt. Not nice is it." Lee shook his head, muttering 'disgusting' under his breath.

"So that just leaves us with two," said Agnes, "both Crispins, Lizzie, and Charles. Let's do Lizzie first."

Lizzie looked up. "The thing I don't understand, Anne," she said, pausing briefly, "is that your problem with that lot goes back years. You and I have never worked in the same team, we never went to the same school, and apart from working here, we have nothing in common. You've been doing Secret Santa for years, so why me this time and why now?"

Anne swivelled on her chair to look at Lizzie.

"It's the same answer for both. You're right, everyone else here and me, we go back years. I never forgot what they did, but I didn't used to dwell on it until recently. A few months ago I was in here, in the canteen getting some lunch and I heard a group of newish employees comparing notes about Lee, Daniel, and Alice. All three of them up to their same old tricks, nothing had changed, and it made me feel sick. Some of those new employees had even tried to raise it, speaking to their managers…" Anne looked at Richard, "or speaking to HR…" At this point, Richard started to wonder if a career in HR was really his 'thing'.

"Nothing was done about it. They were allowed to get away with it over and over again. So I thought I'd raise it with you, Lizzie, a member of the family and a member of the board."

"Why not me?" asked Charles. "You're my assistant, we've always got on well and I've always thought of you as one of the family, so why not me or even Ellen?"

"You didn't want to know about the emails or the sabotage. You brushed them under the carpet so I knew there was no point coming to you as you wouldn't be interested in this either."

Charles suddenly felt the enormity of the year's events catch up with him. He felt ashamed and crushed by his failure to live up to the value he held so dear of 'people'.

"But why target me, Anne, and not HR?" asked Lizzie.

"I told you everything that had been going on, what had happened to me and what was happening to the newbies, but you didn't want to know. You weren't interested. Told me I was being stupid and that the company had policies in place to deal with any issues and if there really had been a problem, it would have been dealt with. You made me so angry with your indifference that I felt like I was burning with rage, so I thought you should too. That burning lipstick from the joke shop was simply perfect for you. I enjoyed it very much."

Before Lizzie could speak, Charles looked up at Agnes and Delores.

"All of these incidents were raised to HR, and nothing happened?" he asked.

Agnes nodded. "You have all these policies in place because you're such a 'people' company, but you don't actually do anything when someone raises a problem. There's no point patting yourselves on your backs and telling yourselves how great your company is to work for if you don't actually follow through, though. And even when Ellen tried to talk to you about the events earlier this year... events as we now know, caused by your own family members, you ignored these as well. I'm afraid your problem became a much bigger problem."

Charles looked at Ellen, then Anne, then over at Richard in HR.

"It sounds like we need to make quite a few changes," he said out loud, whilst his inner voice told him 'HR will be one of them'.

Ellen looked over at Anne.

"Why Charles, Anne?" she asked. "You didn't speak to him about any of these events and I get you were feeling frustrated about the lack of seriousness being shown but why a jigsaw saying, 'I know what you did'? Isn't your point that he didn't do anything?"

Anne wouldn't make eye contact with Ellen or Charles.

"I don't get it," said Charles. "From what you said, you seem to have a justifiable (but still not excusable) reason to go after everyone else. But why me? What have I done to you? You said yourself we've... I've... always showed you kindness and support. I gave you all the time you needed after your brother died. So what did I do? The jigsaw puzzle said, 'I know what you did', well, I'm glad you know, because I sure as hell don't."

"This is where we get the final piece in the puzzle," said Agnes. "As you're all aware, the recurring theme this evening has been family. And that's no different here."

"I'm still confused," said Charles. "Genuinely, I have no idea what's happening anymore."

"Crispin Crisps has been around since 1950," said Delores, "a family-run business which considered all employees weren't just employees, but family."

"I'm beginning to really dislike that word," said Charles.

"The wording on the jigsaw," said Delores, "'I know what you did', could have been a light-hearted prank. Maybe you parked in a parent and child bay or dropped a piece of litter; something small, something witnessed by someone who saw what you did."

"Or," said Agnes, "it could be more of a threat and accusation. 'I *know* what you did.'"

"But I haven't done anything," said Charles, "I promise you; I can't think of anything I've done to make Anne want to give me that jigsaw with that wording. For the last time, what do you think I've done?"

Anne shook her head, refusing to speak.

"I think we'll take it from here," said Agnes. "Anne, you were off work for almost a year, weren't you, after your brother's accident and subsequent death?" Anne nodded her head. "It was an unimaginably awful time for you," continued Agnes. "James was your twin brother, so your connection was deeper than a usual sibling relationship. When you cleared his flat you found some files that

James had which contained some research he was doing." Agnes paused and glanced around the seated group. "James had been researching local Norfolk businesses and unbeknownst to you, had been doing some research on Crispin Crisps' history so you were intrigued to find out more."

Delores took over. "But the content wasn't quite what you were expecting, was it?"

Anne shook her head. "No," she whispered.

"Someone, anyone, get to the point," growled Charles.

Agnes and Delores looked at Charles.

"Well, if you insist," said Delores.

"You're Anne and James's father," said Agnes.

A range of emotions could be seen on Charles's face. Disbelieving. Shock. Bewilderment. Back to disbelieving, then various stages of angry.

"Don't be stupid," he said. "That's the most ludicrous thing I've heard all evening. Absolute rubbish."

On hearing what Agnes said, Ellen, Lizzie and Charlie had also given sharp intakes of breath and gasped.

"What!"

"No!"

"Hilarious!"

"I am *not* the father of Anne or her brother," said Charles. "I'd never met her before she started working here," he said indignantly. "I have no idea why you'd think such utter rubbish."

Anne began to sob. She looked at Charles.

"You are my father… *you are*," and pointing at Agnes and Delores, she said, "and I suspect they can prove it."

"Utter rubbish," repeated Charles.

"You are... you are... you are," cried an emotional Anne before taking a breath then continuing. "Our mother died a few years back; she brought us up on her own, so we never knew our family history. James and I always planned to try and find out where we came from, but he never told me when he was alive what he'd found or been working on. When our mother died, we cleared out her stuff together and he found a load of old papers which went back years and years; I never thought they were very interesting, so I let him keep the lot. But when I started going through his research and our mother's papers, he'd found evidence of payments in there from you."

"Payments? What payments?" spluttered Charles. "I don't know anything about payments. Payments for what? Certainly not from me."

He turned to Ellen. "You're in charge of finance. Was it you?"

"Certainly not," said Ellen. "This is just as much new news to me as it is to you." Ellen looked at Delores.

"Where's your proof of all of this?"

"Bear with us, Ellen, and we'll explain everything."

Agnes looked at Charles and continued.

"James found in their mother's paperwork receipts for regular payments to her from Crispin Crisps. He also found letters from a solicitor confirming that their maternal grandparents accepted the money in return for leaving Norfolk and moving away."

"Her grandparents?" asked Charles. "When the hell were you even born?"

"1971," said Anne. Charles did some mental sums.

"...1971... I was sixteen years old, and I still have no idea what this is all about."

"All this time," said Anne, "and you still deny it. You didn't want to know when my mother told you she was pregnant, and you don't want to know now."

"I have no idea who your mother was," said Charles. "I don't know what you're talking about, and I don't know why anyone in this company was making payments to your grandparents and I have no idea who your real father is, but I can assure you, it *isn't* me."

Agnes looked at Anne.

"I'm afraid, Anne, that Charles really doesn't have a clue what you're talking about."

Agnes turned back to Charles.

"Absolutely, you were sixteen in 1971. Still at school, about to start your A levels, but as can happen even back then, sometimes school kids get a bit too friendly, a bit too overamorous. And one day a girl finds out she's pregnant. And that's what happened to Anne's mother – Wendy Bell."

Charles remained confused. His school days were a long time ago and he didn't remember anyone by that name.

"When Wendy told her parents she was pregnant they weren't best pleased. They never confronted you, but they did come to the factory, and they spoke to your father, Charles Crispin II and your grandfather, Charles I. Between them, they came up with a plan to relocate Wendy and parents from the area and with a generous financial payment until the child turned sixteen."

Delores took over. '*The* child turned out to be twins.

James born first followed by Anne two minutes later. Wendy never told them about you, Charles, or Crispin Crisps. It was pure coincidence that Anne moved back to Norfolk and got a job here." Anne nodded her head, and Delores continued. "Judging by Anne's Internet search history I don't think she's known herself for a hugely long amount of time... am I right?"

Anne nodded. "It was earlier this year when I felt able to start properly going through James's paperwork. All the banking and legal stuff was sorted at the time I started looking at his folders full of research at the start of the year."

"When Anne found out the truth, her world collapsed beneath her. She had lost her mother *and* brother and thought she was all alone. Then she discovered you weren't just a work family but her actual blood family," said Agnes.

"But why not say anything when you found out?" asked Charles. "Why wait until Secret Santa?"

Anne looked at Charles.

"I found out in July but didn't get confirmation until August. I did plan on saying something, but I saw how you reacted when Ellen tried to get you to take seriously the events of this year and I began to see you in a different light. You weren't the kind, gentle, compassionate man I'd known as my boss. I couldn't decide whether to say anything or not but when Lizzie was so horrible to me when I tried to tell her how people really behave here, I snapped and decided that my half-sister and my father would both get an unexpected surprise at Christmas."

"Hang on a moment," said Charlie, "even I will admit this is all a bit fanciful. How do we know any of this is true? Anyone back then could accuse someone of being the father, especially someone from a rich family. Where's the proof? We could be victims of extortion for all you know."

"He's got a point," said Ellen. "You said you have proof, so what is it? How do you know any of this is true?"

Agnes reached for a folder behind her.

"The proof's in here. DNA proof that Charles and Anne are a father and daughter match. When we came in on your Christmas bazaar day, we kept the cups you drank from for fingerprint checking which showed as we now know, Anne was the Secret Santa Slayer. At the time, we couldn't see an obvious reason why Charles was a victim until we saw Anne's Internet history. We then used the cups and some of your hair strands they both left when trying on some of Delores's hats to run a DNA test. We have some contacts who can get samples run at a lab in Norfolk. They search for the tiniest amounts of DNA and magnify them to test. If you didn't know, DNA in our cells are long strands of genetic code, made up of four building blocks, A, C, T and G. The lab has to break down the cell membrane to release the DNA and salt helps those strands stick together. We don't get your whole genome, but the lab looks for A, C, T and G strings in repeating patterns in the chromosomes."

Delores continued. "There are twenty-three pairs of chromosomes, one set from your mother and one set from your father, so forty-six in total. Zero matches means not related, but six matches means a parent, child or sibling match. A fifty percent DNA match confirms father and child, and yes, in this case Charles and Anne matched.

And a twenty-five percent DNA match means half-sibling. To start with, we thought the same as Ellen – that the email hacker, the saboteur and Secret Santa were one and the same person; it made sense for one person to have a vendetta and try as many things as they could to make their point. Lizzie was the first where the fingerprints matched the sabotage, so we focused on her but when the wrapping paper fingerprints pointed straight at Anne, we began to look a bit deeper."

"Once we found that Anne and Charles were a match, we compared Anne to Ellen. This came back as no match, so we tried Anne to Lizzie, which came back as a half-sibling match. We then tried our luck with one of those genealogy websites," said Delores, "you know the ones where you send off a sample and they tell you the breakdown of your ethnicity and match you with long-lost relatives. They're ninety-nine percent accurate so a good comparison for what we found. Well, imagine our surprise when we found that Charlie had done one of these tests and uploaded his results. It pinged straight away as a familial match to Anne."

Charlie looked horrified to learn he'd helped confirm the existence of a half-sister.

"We did a search of the factory one weekend and we found James's research in Anne's desk. It was possibly a bit careless to leave it in an unlocked desk, but it worked to our advantage. Once we got the name of the solicitors, we were able to get some information from them and we also cross-referenced public and financial records," said Delores.

"We went back in time and checked the fiscal history

of the accounts submitted for Crispin Crisps," said Agnes, "and we could see regular payments made for eighteen years into a trust fund in Wendy Bell's and her parents' names. So, Ellen… Charlie… we do have proof. But Charles is also right; he didn't know. His father and grandfather kept it from him." Agnes paused before looking at Anne. "Anne… I'm sorry… but Charles really had no idea you were his daughter."

There was a brief silence.

"I didn't know," said Charles, almost whispering. "I didn't know… I don't know what to say." He looked into Anne's eyes. "I promise you I didn't know. They never told me."

Anne was also in a state of shock.

"I thought you knew," she said. "I thought you didn't want anything to do with us and just pretended we didn't exist. When I found out the truth, I kept asking myself why you didn't recognise me, how a father could not know his own daughter." Charles could do no more than shrug his shoulders, his mind buzzing with a million thoughts. He then looked over at Delores and Agnes.

"So the final piece of the puzzle really is the jigsaw puzzle. Everything tonight, everything from Karen, Lizzie, Charlie and Anne comes back to it and what it said."

"Ah," said Delores, "not quite the final piece."

"There can't be any more," said Charles. "Everything's in tatters now, broken to pieces – no more – please, I beg you."

"When you put a jigsaw together, that final piece, whether it's a 100-, 500- or even a 10,000- piece jigsaw, that final piece brings the whole picture to life," said Agnes.

"Once we found out that Anne was a Crispin we wanted to make sure we had all the pieces in place. But we were missing that final piece, so we had a deeper look at the legal documentation regarding Crispin Crisps."

"Not another kid," sniped Charlie.

"No, not another child," said Agnes.

"So what is it then? What did you find out?" asked Ellen, although somewhat nervously based on everything she'd already heard tonight.

Delores looked at Ellen and said, "It's probably best now to bring Jayne in from a legal standpoint to explain this one."

Jayne, who had been very quiet throughout the entire evening's events, now took her place in front of the semicircle.

"I've gone back through every single legal document in relation to the set-up of Crispin Crisps. Every piece, and I do mean every piece of paper going back to 1950 when the company was first created and then every document and transfer of ownership records when the next heir took over."

"Big deal," said Charlie, "no surprises there; the business always goes to the son of the current owner. So that makes it me next and quite frankly, the sooner the better."

"The problem though," said Jayne, "is that the documentation does not reference the oldest *legitimate* son. The papers are very clear; the legal covenant only states the 'first born son', it does not say 'legitimate first son through marriage'. Whether it was worded badly or maybe at the time the company was founded it was just a natural assumption that future generations of children would always be legitimate, we'll never know. But in black and white terms, legal terms, the oldest son inherits. It means, Charlie, that if James were still alive, he would have inherited the company, not you."

Charlie looked appalled and very angry.

"Not a problem. He's dead so it changes nothing, the business will be mine." Charles clenched his right fist and fought the urge to stand up and punch his son into the middle of the new year.

"It changes everything," he said.

"The business should have been James's birthright, not yours," said Anne.

"So the meaning of 'I know what you did. You will pay,'" said Charles, "meant that you thought I got your mother pregnant, walked away from her and ignored you and James? Then pretended you didn't exist so Charlie would inherit?"

Anne simply said, "Yes."

"And that," said Delores, "was the final piece of the puzzle. Everything that there was to know is known. Everything is out in the open, whether you like it or not."

For a brief moment, no one spoke.

"So what do we do now?" asked Charles, breaking the silence. "We've heard some pretty awful things tonight."

"What happens next," said Agnes, "well, I'm afraid, that's entirely up to you. We've done our job and found out who was acting with malicious intent. Admittedly a bit of a surprise to find it wasn't just one person, but three, plus one who happily took the blame until tonight."

"We also checked the police file in Yarmouth," said

Delores. "Ellen, you only reported the Secret Santa incidents, so they concluded it was just an employee playing a joke. 'An internal matter for the company to deal with' was their conclusion. Maybe if you'd called them at the start of the year when the emails began, they might have taken it a bit more seriously and prevented everything else, but all they had to go on were a few people getting silly gifts in a Secret Santa."

"So as far as the police are concerned, this is your internal matter to deal with," said Agnes. "For what it's worth, I think you've got a lot to talk about and a lot to change. Starting with your family and then how the factory is run. But ultimately, it's up to you. Change or don't change, it's entirely your choice."

"I wish I'd listened earlier," said Charles and turning to Ellen he said, "I'm so sorry."

Ellen gave him a smile back and reached out to take his hand. Charles then looked back at Agnes and Delores.

"I suppose I should say thank you to you."

"Not if you don't want to," said Agnes. "Either way, our bill's in the post and it's a big one."

Ellen silently mouthed the words 'thank you' to Delores.

Agnes and Delores picked up their belongings.

"We'll be off now. You've all got an awful lot to think and talk about, so we'll leave you to it. It's been one hell of a night," said Delores.

"Think carefully before you do anything rash because it'll impact more than just you lot sitting here right now," said Agnes and with that she and Delores left the canteen and made their way down to the outer doors.

As they got into the fresh December air, they shivered. It must have been nearly midnight by now and it was freezing cold, almost New Year's Eve.

"I don't know about you, Agnes, but I could do with a cup of tea and something to eat," said Delores.

Agnes agreed. "Too right, a nice hot cup of tea would go down really well right now, but on the something to eat front, maybe not crisps."

Delores looked at Agnes. "Definitely not crisps."

THE END

OR MAYBE NOT…

Both Agnes and Delores had switched their mobile phones to silent when they arrived at the Crispin Crisps factory, and neither of them had thought to check their phones throughout the evening, nor when they left.

If they had, they would have seen five missed calls on both their devices, plus three WhatsApp messages on the detective agency chat. Message one read, 'URGENT! More items stolen', message two read, 'CALL ME' and message three read, 'This is Armadillo. Call me'.

To be continued…

This book is printed on paper from sustainable sources managed under the Forest Stewardship Council (FSC) scheme.

It has been printed in the UK to reduce transportation miles and their impact upon the environment.

For every new title that Troubador publishes, we plant a tree to offset CO_2, partnering with the More Trees scheme.

For more about how Troubador offsets its environmental impact, see www.troubador.co.uk/sustainability-and-community